The Passionate POWERS

*Men bound by blood, tied to the sea
and destined to be heroes.*

Meet the Powers men:

Jackson Powers. Maritime lawyer. Rich, handsome and *stranded with baby* in *A Bride for Jackson Powers* by Dixie Browning, a 2/00 Silhouette Desire title.

Matthew Powers. Sea captain, forefather. Strong, honorable and *married for convenience* in *The Paper Marriage* by Bronwyn Williams, an 8/00 Harlequin Historicals novel.

Curt Powers. Navy SEAL. Arresting, determined and *involved in a dangerous mission of the most private nature* in *The Virgin and the Vengeful Groom* by Dixie Browning, an 11/00 Silhouette Desire title.

**Don't miss this exciting new series from
Silhouette Desire and Harlequin Historicals!**

Dear Reader,

In keeping with the celebration of Silhouette's 20th anniversary in 2000, what better way to enjoy the new century's first Valentine's Day than to read six passionate, powerful, provocative love stories from Silhouette Desire!

Beloved author Dixie Browning returns to Desire's MAN OF THE MONTH promotion with *A Bride for Jackson Powers,* also the launch title for the series THE PASSIONATE POWERS. Enjoy this gem about a single dad who becomes stranded with a beautiful widow who's his exact opposite.

Get ready to be seduced when Alexandra Sellers offers you another sheikh hero from her SONS OF THE DESERT miniseries with *Sheikh's Temptation.* Maureen Child's popular series BACHELOR BATTALION continues with *The Daddy Salute*—a marine turns helpless when he must take care of his baby, and he asks the heroine for help.

Kate Little brings you a keeper with *Husband for Keeps,* in which the heroine needs an in-name-only husband in order to hold on to her ranch. A fabulously sexy doctor returns to the woman he could never forget in *The Magnificent M.D.* by Carol Grace. And exciting newcomer Sheri WhiteFeather offers another irresistible Native American hero in *Jesse Hawk: Brave Father.*

We hope you will indulge yourself this Valentine's Day with all six of these passionate romances, only from Silhouette Desire!

Enjoy!

Joan Marlow Golan

Joan Marlow Golan
Senior Editor, Silhouette Desire

Please address questions and book requests to:
Silhouette Reader Service
U.S.: 3010 Walden Ave., P.O. Box 1325, Buffalo, NY 14269
Canadian: P.O. Box 609, Fort Erie, Ont. L2A 5X3

A Bride for Jackson Powers

DIXIE BROWNING

Silhouette

Desire

Published by Silhouette Books

America's Publisher of Contemporary Romance

For Curtiss Ann Matlock, my dearest friend,
distant cousin and Oklahoma connection.
We've put in a few airport hours together, too.

SILHOUETTE BOOKS

ISBN 0-373-76273-9

A BRIDE FOR JACKSON POWERS

Visit us at www.romance.net

Printed in U.S.A.

DIXIE BROWNING

celebrated her sixty-fifth book for Silhouette with the publication of *Texas Millionaire* in 1999. She has also written a number of historical romances with her sister under the name Bronwyn Williams. A charter member of Romance Writers of America, and a member of Novelists, Inc., Dixie has won numerous awards for her work. She lives on the Outer Banks of North Carolina.

IT'S OUR 20th ANNIVERSARY!
We'll be celebrating all year, continuing with these fabulous titles, on sale in February 2000.

Special Edition

#1303 Man...Mercenary...Monarch
Joan Elliott Pickart

#1304 Dr. Mom and the Millionaire
Christine Flynn

#1305 Who's That Baby?
Diana Whitney

#1306 Cattleman's Courtship
Lois Faye Dyer

#1307 The Marriage Basket
Sharon De Vita

#1308 Falling for an Older Man
Trisha Alexander

Intimate Moments

#985 The Wildes of Wyoming—Chance
Ruth Langan

#986 Wild Ways
Naomi Horton

#987 Mistaken Identity
Merline Lovelace

#988 Family on the Run
Margaret Watson

#989 On Dangerous Ground
Maggie Price

#990 Catch Me If You Can
Nina Bruhns

Romance

#1426 Waiting for the Wedding
Carla Cassidy

#1427 Bringing Up Babies
Susan Meier

#1428 The Family Diamond
Moyra Tarling

#1429 Simon Says...Marry Me!
Myrna Mackenzie

#1430 The Double Heart Ranch
Leanna Wilson

#1431 If the Ring Fits...
Melissa McClone

Desire

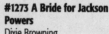

#1273 A Bride for Jackson Powers
Dixie Browning

#1274 Sheikh's Temptation
Alexandra Sellers

#1275 The Daddy Salute
Maureen Child

#1276 Husband for Keeps
Kate Little

#1277 The Magnificent M.D.
Carol Grace

#1278 Jesse Hawk: Brave Father
Sheri WhiteFeather

One

Obviously, Jackson was doing it all wrong. He didn't even know how to hold her. You'd think a man his age would've learned that much by now. She'd started to squeal and kick him in the belly.

A few people glared at him. Most were too busy comparing hard-luck stories.

"...catch a shuttle. If I'm not in D.C. by nine tomorrow—"

"Fat chance. I've been standing here for the past three hours and the damned line hasn't moved an inch, I swear."

"This place stinks. I mean literally! Last time I'm ever going to plan a trip this time of year, so help me. Hey, quit shoving, will you?"

Two small boys broke through the line, whooping like wild animals. A middle-aged woman wearing sweats and a fur coat dropped a heap of carry-on luggage, flopped down on the pile and began to swear.

Jax wanted to say, Yeah, well what if you were stuck here with a daughter you'd met only hours earlier, who doesn't even speak the damned language? He sniffed. He had a pretty good idea what was stinking, and it wasn't just the weather. He jiggled the damp, squirming baby in his arms, mumbling words that were supposed to be comforting, but didn't appear to have that effect. Too bad babies didn't come with an operations manual.

Someone bumped him from behind and murmured a soft apology. The natives were getting restless. He'd heard of road rage. It was nothing compared to airport rage, given a holiday crowd and the ice storm of the century.

"Whaddya mean, flight delayed? I gotta get outta here, dammit!" the man in front of him shouted. "Don't nobody in this place know how to deice a plane? Buncha idiots, if you ask me!"

Lines for the two flights serviced from this particular desk had already merged into one unruly mob. He was being jostled from all sides.

The sigh that came from behind him was almost lost in the clamor. Jax's shoulders sagged as Sunny shifted from fret mode to shriek mode. Pink-shod feet, size zilch, kicked him in the belly. Poor kid must be miserable. He wondered how long it would take the dampness to soak through her padded pink snowsuit and all the layers it enclosed.

Another sigh whispered behind him. He was tempted to turn around and snap out something really helpful, like, "You think *you've* got troubles? How'd you like to try mine on for size?"

He shifted his burden, struggling to hold on to baby, briefcase, carrier and pink plastic diaper bag. Sunny was bored with the carrier, which was why he was carrying her in his arms. The thing was a damned nuisance, but Carolyn had said she needed it.

"Shh, yeah, I know, babe, it's a rough deal. I'll get us out of here, don't worry." At this point he'd gladly take the first flight out, regardless of where it was bound.

"Excuse me," said a voice so soft he nearly missed it.

"You talking to me?" He turned to the woman behind him in what had once been an orderly line.

"I was wondering—do you know—I mean, I think your baby might need changing."

"So?" He wasn't normally given to surliness, but these were not normal circumstances. "Sorry. Yeah, I kind of suspected as much."

The woman glanced around, probably searching for someone who looked like a wife and mother. There were plenty of likely looking candidates as far as age was concerned, only none of them belonged to him and Sunny.

"Um…maybe I could hold your place in line while you…uh…"

"Change her drawers? You mean right *here?*" Jax dodged as a utility cart beeped its way through the throng.

"I'm pretty sure I saw a changing table in the ladies' room."

"The ladies' room. Now, why didn't I think of that?" Jax's conscience was broadsided by a pair of silver-gray eyes the size of half dollars. Sarcasm wasn't going to help matters. Besides, she didn't deserve it, she was only trying to help.

It was the first thing he noticed about her, after the voice. Those eyes. Because it beat staring at the foul-mouthed fathead in front of him, he took a moment to size up the rest. Either she was an elegant idiot or a model fresh off a tropical assignment. At first glance, her face struck him as too thin to be called pretty. Her skinny skirt, splashed with big, colorful blossoms, came down to her ankles and was topped off with a few baggy layers that wouldn't stand a chance against this weather. He hoped to hell she had something warmer stashed away in a locker. That yellow thing draped around her shoulders wasn't going to do the job.

"Look, I'm really sorry, miss. I know you're only trying to—" Suddenly Sunny lunged. The woman flung up her hands in an instinctive gesture to catch her.

"I guess she's hungry, too," Jax said, a note of desperation edging into his voice. "I offered her a bottle, but she wasn't interested.'' He bounced the baby some more, the only noticeable effect of which was to make her pitiful cries waver.

Where was his secretary when he needed her?

Where was Sunny's mother when he needed her?

Hell, for that matter, where was any woman when a man really needed them? One thing he'd learned over the course of nearly four decades was that women were about as dependable as the weather. Nothing had ever happened to change his mind to any great degree.

''This damned ice gets any thicker,'' the guy in front grumbled, ''we won't get out of here till the Fourth of July. Where the hell is all this global warming when you need it, somebody wanna tell me that?''

Jackson Powers, who answered to Jax, J.M. and Mr. Powers, came close to regretting the impulse that had made him race directly from his office to Norfolk International, where he'd taken a seat on the first plane headed west. Thank God he kept a razor and a toothbrush at his office. He'd stuffed those and the report he'd been working on into his briefcase.

When he'd gotten the call from Carolyn Tribble, a woman with whom he'd had a short, pleasant fling out in San Diego about a year and a half ago, he'd been in the middle of negotiating the case of the single-hulled tanker, Panamanian registry, that had sunk off the Jersey coast back in October and was threatening the entire area with a massive oil spill. It had taken him a couple of minutes to place her.

''Jackson, this is probably going to come as a surprise,'' she'd said, ''but you have a six-month-old daughter.''

Surprise? Try stunned disbelief. Try instinctive denial. He never took chances when it came to sex. ''What makes you think it's mine?'' he asked cautiously.

''Well, hon, the timing, for one thing. You were the only man I slept with after I filed for divorce. I was real careful about that because Stu was having me followed. Anyway, right after you flew back east I came down with this flu thing that dragged on for weeks, and sex was the last thing I was interested in, so you see, she has to be yours. That's why I put your name on her birth certificate. Besides, she's got your forehead and all that thick black hair, and I'm a natural blonde, remember? We talked about it that night I—''

''Look, are you sure about this? I always take precautions.''

''Remember that night in the bathtub, when you got that big bruise on your—''

''Okay, so maybe we slipped up once, but—''

''Slipped down, actually. It's a wonder we didn't break our necks. And it was twice, in case you've forgotten the next morning. That's when we saw your bruise, remember?''

There was a long silence, during which Jax tried to recall the details of the encounter in question.

''Um…a daughter, you say.'' His mind had raced frantically, weaving the shocking news into a totally unrelated memory from the distant past. ''Carolyn?

You still there? Look, how about if we got married? I know it's a little late, but—''

''Oh, Jackson, you are so *sweet!* Thanks, but no thanks. That's just what I'd have expected from you, though. You're a genuine throwback, a real gentleman. What I was sort of hoping was that you'd already have a wife by now, and maybe you and she could…you know, like maybe adopt her? I mean, Sunny's my baby, too, after all, and I do want the best for her.''

''A daughter. I have a daughter,'' he remembered repeating numbly, unable to absorb the impact.

She had gone on to tell him all her reasons for not having an abortion, and how she'd honestly intended to be a wonderful mother, but that was before she'd become seriously involved with this guy from the State Department. ''So you see, I'll be traveling all over Europe the next few years, doing a lot of entertaining, and a baby's not going to fit into that kind of life-style. What Sunny needs is two loving parents and a real home. Jax, that's absolutely the only reason I'm putting her up for adoption, because she's a perfect doll. You'll adore her. Everyone does.''

He started to speak, but she wasn't finished. ''So I thought I'd give you first choice, but if you can't take her, I won't have any trouble finding someone to adopt her. In that case, though, I'll still need your signature.''

That was Carolyn. Strikingly attractive, highly intelligent, totally self-centered. He wasn't sure he could tolerate being married to her, but for the sake of their child he'd been willing to give it a shot.

So now here he was, stuck in a socked-in airport in Chicago on his way back to Norfolk with a baby that had his forehead and his thick black hair.

Jax's hair was straight and laced with gray, while Sunny's was soft as down and curly, but one look at that small pink face and he'd known. Known it in the marrow of his bones, or wherever such knowledge was centered. She was his, all right—toothless grin, fat pink cheeks, navy-blue eyes and all. His daughter.

"I could take her for you."

"Huh?" His attention swerved to the tall, thin woman with the clear gray eyes and the quiet voice.

"Into the ladies' room, I mean. To change her diaper. You could stand guard outside the door if you're worried. Not that I'd blame you, because you read about things every day—kidnappings and all, I mean. And I'm a stranger, so it pays to be cautious."

Caution fought with desperation. Desperation won. "Shh, Sunny, it's going to be all right." After only a moment's hesitation, Jax handed his daughter over to the woman in the long, flowered skirt, the thick-heeled sandals and the layers of baggy sweaters on top. He was no expert on women's fashions. Most of the women he associated with in the course of his work wore tailored suits. As for the others—the ones he took to dinner, a show, and occasionally to bed—they always looked pretty, but he'd never spent much time analyzing what they wore.

"Yeah, if you wouldn't mind, I guess she'd be

more comfortable. There's powder and diapers and stuff in here—'' He handed over the large pink bag and the carrier, then braced himself to wait. ''Her name's Sunny,'' he called as an afterthought.

He could only hope he was doing the right thing. What he knew about babies could be scratched on the head of a thumbtack.

His daughter. That red-faced, smelly, noisy little miracle was his own flesh and blood. God, he didn't know the first thing about relating to family. Other than the great-uncle a social worker had tracked down some thirty-five years ago who'd installed him in a series of boarding schools and grudgingly paid the freight, he'd never had to deal with a family. At least not since he was six years old.

As she turned away from the darkly handsome creature with the stern face, the guarded eyes and the beard-shadowed jaw, Hetty's arms curved around the soggy little bundle. Brushing her lips against a soft, dark curl, she whispered, ''Don't fuss, sugar-britches, he'll be right there waiting for you when I get you all cleaned up.''

He didn't quite trust her, that much was obvious, but what choice had he had? If it hadn't been for the hint of vulnerability he'd let slip through his guard, Hetty would never in a million years have dared speak to him. Mercy, he was intimidating. But at least he seemed to care about the baby, which said a lot in his favor.

Edging her way through the cluster of women, she

got in line for one of the changing tables. The line inched forward slowly. Hetty bounced a fretful Sunny in her arms, wondering what on earth had possessed her to do such a thing. She had her own problems to deal with without taking on someone else's burden. She'd been on her way from Oklahoma to Miami, Florida, supposedly changing planes in Cincinnati and again in Atlanta, when her plans had started to fall apart.

A table opened up and she grabbed it, plopping her charge down on her padded backside. "Stop squirming, sugar, your little doohickey's stuck." She struggled with the zipper, half-afraid if she took too long the baby's father would come after her. "Ooh, you're a real mess, aren't you?" Rummaging in the stuffed diaper bag, she found a container of predampened tissues. "No wonder you were so fussy, you're getting a rash."

Holding two wriggling feet up with one hand, she felt in the bag again with the other and came up with a familiar-looking tube. She'd used the same ointment on Robert whenever he'd been threatened with diaper rash.

"I hope you've got a teething ring in here somewhere, else you're going to wear those knuckles out," she murmured. There were already several women lined up behind her, waiting for the fold-down changing table. The rest room was crowded. Someone called out that there was no paper. A roll was tossed from one booth to the other.

Mercy, to think she'd harbored the illusion that

travel would be one glamorous adventure after another. Her friend at the agency had explained that the cheapest rates involved an illogical route with several changes along the way. Hetty hadn't been intimidated. Once she'd taken the first step, she hadn't looked back.

Now she almost wished she had. Still, her very first flight was proving exciting, if a bit tiresome. And in a few hours she'd be embarking on her very first cruise.

"Here's hoping I don't have to change ships between islands," she muttered, disposing of the soiled diaper.

At any other time in her life, Hetty would never have considered doing something so absurdly impractical, never mind expensive. But when an old friend, a woman who knew about her situation and who worked at a travel agency in Oklahoma City, had called to tell her about a last-minute cancellation, Hetty had jumped at the chance. It was too late now for second thoughts.

"There, sweetheart, we're all done. Let's see if Papa brought along something for you to eat, shall we?"

"Would you *mind?* You're not the only mother with a wet kid."

Hetty smiled apologetically. "We're all finished. Sorry you had to wait." She got a frown for her efforts and scurried out of the way, taking her place in the line waiting for a lavatory.

The familiar scent of baby oil and the feel of the

small, sweet bundle in her arms brought back painful memories. Hetty promised herself resolutely that once she got back from her cruise, found a job and a place to live, she would begin mending fences. Family— any sort of family at all—was too precious to be squandered. She was determined to patch things up again.

Conscious of the waiting lines behind her, she spared only a fleeting glance in the mirror, startled all over again by her new haircut and the unfamiliar clothes. If she'd known she was going to wind up in ice-bound Chicago instead of balmy Miami, she would have dressed far differently. Or at least worn something warmer than the silky knit tunic, the overshirt and shawl the clerk assured her were made to be worn with the new longer skirts.

But there'd been no way of knowing that the jet stream would zig when it should have zagged, or that the arctic blast would collide with a stream of Gulf moisture along the mid-Atlantic.

Hundreds of flights were being diverted as, one after another, airports from Atlanta northward were shutting down. Evidently she was among the lucky ones. According to rumor, there were a number of loaded flights trapped on runways, unable to take off, unable to return to the gates because of the planes already stranded there.

From now on, she'd just as soon stick to Greyhound.

With the diaper bag and carrier in one hand, and her big, lightweight purse that was supposed to be just the thing for traveling over her shoulder, she hugged the infant who was chewing on her yellow fringed shawl and said, "Come on, sugar-britches, let's go before your daddy sends out a search party."

He was hovering like a dark cloud just outside the ladies' room door. Hetty wondered if he was even aware of all the women who glanced at him and then turned back for a second look.

Probably used to it. He was that kind of man. George Clooney with a harder edge, a narrower backside and broader shoulders. She'd noticed that much standing in line behind him, before she'd ever seen his face, which seemed to wear a perpetual scowl.

"About time you showed up. I was starting to worry."

The crowd was thicker than ever, and from the snatches of conversation, growing more impatient by the minute. "Sorry. These things take time. Your little girl's got a rash, and she's either hungry or teething or both, but at least she's dry now."

Reluctantly she handed the baby to her father, thinking about the baby she'd left behind. As long as she was going to have to find work quickly once she got back home, she might as well try something in the care-giving line. At least she'd had plenty of experience.

She'd hoped the weather might have miraculously cleared while she was inside. It hadn't. Fortunately she still had plenty of time to reach Miami.

Smiling, she gave the baby a goodbye pat on her

padded bottom and said, "This isn't the way the travel ads described it, else I might not have tried it."

"Tried what?"

"Flying." Sunny snuggled into her father's arms and began to gnaw on his collar. The man was a mess. An expensive-looking suede jacket was slung over one shoulder, his tie was loose, the two top buttons on his shirt unfastened. Hetty thought she'd never seen a more strikingly attractive man in her life, scowl and all.

The scowl moderated. "You mean you've never flown before?"

"I never needed to go anywhere farther than Oklahoma City."

"You picked a lousy time for your maiden voyage."

"I'm beginning to—" Someone struck her in the back, and she stumbled against the man and baby. His free arm came around her, the carrier and diaper bag slammed into her behind, and she inhaled sharply, absorbing the mingled scent of bergamot and leather.

It occurred to her that with spare time on her hands for the first time in her adult life, she might just weave herself a lovely romantic fantasy from this chance encounter.

The fantasy gripped her arm and growled in her ear. "Let's get out of this mob."

Startled, Hetty glanced around. If there was a place out of the flow of traffic, it must be a closely guarded secret. Children played reckless games of tag or whined and tugged at parents' arms. Babies cried.

Tired travelers tried to hang on to baggage, children and patience against a constantly shifting current of humanity. Over all that came the confusing din of weather updates, distorted loudspeaker announcements and the polite beep-beep of motorized carts on some mysterious mission of their own.

Such was the power of a well-directed scowl, that Sunny's father was able to lead her through the throng to a relatively clear corner behind a deserted service desk. "Hold her while I shift these trash receptacles, will you?"

Hetty watched as he rearranged airport property, commandeering an abandoned wheelchair and using it to block off a six-square-foot fortress. "Can you do that?" she asked dubiously.

The look he shot her said, I did it, didn't I? Who are you to question my authority?

Hetty sighed. She might look like a seasoned traveler in her brand-new outfit, the discount store's version of resort wear, but underneath it all she was plain-old Henrietta Reynolds, a thirty-seven-year old widow, who had never traveled farther than a few hundred miles from home in her life.

"I guess we'd better introduce ourselves. Jax Powers," he said, extending a square, masculine hand. His dark-blue eyes still had that guarded look, as if he weren't sure he was doing the right thing, encouraging a chance-met stranger.

Hetty shifted the baby and clasped his dry, hard palm with her own. "Hetty Reynolds. I notice you call your daughter—she is your daughter, I believe you said? And you call her…Sonny?''

''She is my daughter, and that's Sunny with a *U*, not an *O*. Miss Marilyn Carolyn Powers.''

Her mouth formed a silent *O*.

He shrugged. ''Yeah, I know. I was told she answers to Sunny. It'll do for now.'' Before Hetty could think of a response, he said, ''Look, I don't know about you, but I'm getting hungry. Could I leave you two here while I go find us some supper or lunch or whatever's available?''

''Food. Mercy, I didn't realize it, but I haven't eaten since I left home, if you don't count pretzels.''

''Stay right here.''

As if she would dare do anything else. Behind the impromptu barrier there was no place to sit except the floor. She sat, settling Sunny on her lap and plopping purse and diaper bag in the carrier. She'd located a crushed box of teething biscuits under the diapers, as well as two jars of pears and one of squash, four cans of formula and two nursing bottles.

''At least you won't starve, sugar-bun.'' Secure in her tiny fortress, she hummed snatches of several lullabies as she watched the parade of fellow travelers. Despite the unexpected delay, it was all still new enough to be exciting.

Occasionally she glanced at her watch, forcing out any encroaching doubts by concentrating on the future.

For years she'd been far too busy to waste time on

daydreams. Oddly enough she'd discovered quite recently that when it came to dreaming, she was a natural. For instance, she'd had no trouble at all picturing herself dancing under a tropical moon. Dining on food she hadn't had to cook or serve, from dishes she wouldn't have to wash, surrounded by beautiful, well-dressed people who neither complained nor demanded.

Heaven. It was going to be sheer heaven for seven whole days.

Nearly an hour dragged past before Jax returned with two foam cups and a paper sack. "The situation's not quite desperate yet, but it's not likely to improve until the weather lets up. Latest word is that in another six hours, tops, we'll be on our way."

A wide smile spread over Hetty's face. Not for one moment had she let herself think she wouldn't reach Miami in time. Still, being a novice traveler, she hadn't quite been able to relax.

"Hope you take cream in your coffee and don't mind chili and onions on your dogs. I got us two apiece since this might have to last awhile."

Hetty reached behind her for her purse, but at the look on his face, she murmured her thanks and shifted Sunny to the carrier seat so that she could take the proffered food.

There was something oddly companionable about sitting shoulder to shoulder on a hard, carpeted floor, eating cold hotdogs and drinking weak, lukewarm coffee. Sunny alternately dozed and waked to gum her biscuit, scattering sticky crumbs on Hetty's lap and smearing a few on the sleeve of Jax's tan suede jacket.

They didn't talk much. That suited Hetty just fine. If she'd ever possessed any social skills they had long since withered from lack of practice.

"Do you suppose I could find my way back here if I go wash up?" she asked, neatly tucking her napkin and cup into the grease-stained paper sack.

"Leave a trail of bread crumbs."

"Does a wet teething biscuit qualify as bread crumbs?"

He grinned, and she was struck all over again by what a remarkably attractive man he was. And to think that she, plain old Hetty Reynolds, was sharing time, space and conversation with him. You might even say she was having dinner with him.

He told her to shift the wheelchair, slip through and then roll it back in place. "Take a right, go about fifty feet, cross to the other side and you're there. Reverse the procedure on the way back."

"Easy for you to say," Hetty retorted. She retrieved her purse and set out, dismissing the fear that she wouldn't be able to find her way back through the mob. Or if she did, that the man and his baby would have moved on.

Jax watched her go, weaving gracefully past outstretched limbs and heaps of luggage, stepping over a couple of teenagers sleeping on the floor. She even walked like a model, that subtle sway that hinted at feminine secrets under the loose, formless clothes.

Not that he was any expert on fashion models. For

the most part, the women in his life, at least since his days in the marine corps, were either lawyers or businesswomen. Even those who weren't were no more interested in long-term involvement than he was.

And he definitely wasn't.

Hetty. He couldn't quite figure her out. One corner of one of her incisors was chipped. He found the small flaw strangely intriguing. She might act as if all this was new to her, but he could easily picture her with her head in the air, striding down a runway, her long, limp outfit flapping loosely in a way that subtly emphasized the feminine form underneath.

Don't even think about it, Powers. You've got trouble enough without looking for more.

Two

Hetty yawned. She'd fallen asleep, only to wake up with her head on Jax's shoulder. "I'm really sorry," she murmured. "Your arm must be aching. You should have wakened me."

"No problem."

She smoothed her skirt, pretending a nonchalance she was far from feeling. She'd been married for eleven years, for heaven's sake. When it came to men, she wasn't entirely without experience.

Jax went back to the business section of yesterday's *New York Times.* Sunny was making sucking noises in her sleep. Hetty, needing to do something to counteract her embarrassment, tucked the blanket around the small, chubby body, her hands lingering on the dimpled knees.

"She's awfully good-natured."

"Hmm?"

"Sunny. Her diaper rash is better. As long as her bottom's dry and her stomach's full, she seems content just to watch the world go by."

"Let's hope things get moving around here before we run out of food and diapers."

Rather pointedly, he went back to his newspaper, and Hetty frowned at her watch, then squinted at it to be sure the hands were still moving.

They were. Nothing else was, at least not so far as travel was concerned. The same old mob, moving sluggishly now, if at all. Other than a few snores and a minor fracas now and then, they were quieter. Three rows away, an elderly man was demanding to see someone from security. His wife kept shushing him, telling him everything was going to be all right, that she'd checked their horoscope before they'd left home that morning.

Hetty wondered what her own horoscope had said. Had it mentioned anything about meeting a tall, dark and handsome stranger? If it weren't for Jax she might have been concerned by now, but outright panic was a luxury she'd never been able to afford.

She hadn't panicked back in those miserable days after her mother had died, when her father's drinking had gone from bad to worse. Nor a few years later, when she could no longer convince herself that he was still grieving, that he truly loved her and that he regretted the outbursts, which had grown more and more violent.

Instead she had quietly made plans to move to Oklahoma City as soon as she graduated, to find a job and a place to stay.

She certainly hadn't panicked the day she had stood before the justice of peace and placed her life in the hands of a man more than twice her age, even though he'd been practically a stranger. They'd known each other only in the way most people living in the same small town did. Still, Gus had offered her a safer alternative than running away to the city with no funds, no friends and no job. She would always be grateful to him for that.

She hadn't panicked eleven years later when Gus had flown his plane into a power line and been killed, nor when her mother-in-law had suffered the first in a series of strokes, nor when Jeannie, Gus's teenage daughter, had "borrowed" her credit card and run up an enormous debt just before she dropped out of school and disappeared. Not even when the rebellious fifteen-year-old had come home again five months ago—just long enough to leave her newborn infant.

Hetty had coped with it all. She was not an excitable woman.

Or maybe she'd just never had the luxury of giving in to her emotions.

At any rate, Jax had come along before she had any inkling how bad the weather really was. Thank goodness for that. And for his kindness, his decency, his knowledge.

As for that mysterious quality that made her stomach flutter when he happened to touch her or look at her with one eyebrow slightly elevated, one corner of his gorgeous mouth quirked...

Well. The less she thought about that, the better. That sort of fantasy could wait until she embarked on her cruise.

But first she had to get to Miami. So far as she could tell, nothing was moving outside. As Jeannie would say, it was Sleepy Hollowsville. Minco, the town where they lived, had been Deadsville. Jeannie's school had been Dullsville.

Hetty wondered what her own life had been? Busysville?

Determined to hang on to her optimism, she dug out the dog-eared brochure a friend who had moved to the city and gone to work for a travel agency had mailed her. She gazed at the color photos and reread the copy she'd long since memorized.

"Dining under the stars...dancing on the fan-tail...nightly shows, live music, the adventure of a lifetime."

Yes, well...first she had to get there. Once the weather broke, it shouldn't take long to scrape the runways and deice the planes. She knew about things like that because she'd read practically every adult offering in the library at least once.

As if picking up on her thoughts, Jax laid his paper aside and asked when her cruise was scheduled to leave Miami. He had turned back the sleeves of his gray broadcloth shirt to reveal tanned, muscular fore-arms with a dusting of crisp, dark hairs. His necktie, thoroughly chewed by his daughter, had been crammed into his briefcase.

"I'm supposed to board at four tomorrow afternoon. Thank goodness I allowed extra time and made a room reservation for tonight near the airport there. My friend at the agency suggested it." She chewed on her lower lip. "Do you think I ought to call and tell them to hold it in case I'm late?" She answered her own question. "No, there's no chance of that. Once we're able to leave, it won't take long to get there."

"Have you checked in with your friend to let her know what's happened?"

"Do I need to?"

"It wouldn't hurt."

Jax knew it would mean standing in another line, waiting for a pay phone to be free. He would've offered her his cell phone, but reception was lousy. Too much interference.

He watched her weave her way through the crowd, wondering if she did it deliberately—that slight swing of the shoulders counterbalanced by the subtle sway of her hips.

Probably something to do with bone structure. He was no expert, but even under those limp, floppy layers, hers looked pretty damned fine, from the high forehead, to the delicate cheekbones and elegant neck, right down to those world-class ankles. Not even the clunky sandals could detract from her classy lines.

Beside him, Sunny experimented with a new sound that involved humming and gum smacking. Jax laid a hand on her warm little belly. "Nice friend you've got there, kid. Let's hope we can find you someone just as nice once we get home."

Home. That was another problem to be dealt with. His Norfolk apartment was strictly adults only. Maybe he'd better call his secretary and get her started on lining up a few prospects. A nice house in a quiet neighborhood, with a big yard and a nearby school. While she was at it, she might arrange for him to interview prospective nannies and housekeepers. He'd need one of each.

Still no sign of Hetty. He could go after her, but he didn't particularly want to risk losing their space. Besides, he could easily miss her in this throng. She might even have found somebody else. Teamed up with someone who didn't have a kid needing attention every few minutes.

The idea was surprisingly unwelcome.

Having learned a long time ago not to expect anything from a woman, Jax had seldom been disappointed. He couldn't quite figure this one, though. Something about her didn't add up.

Or was it that the sum total wasn't what he expected of a woman who looked like a model, walked like a model and talked like a small-town housewife from flyover country?

Actually, she didn't talk all that much, which in itself was unusual. Most of the women he knew, especially the beautiful ones, were inclined to chatter.

Dismissing the woman from his mind, he turned his thoughts to the domino effect the addition of one small daughter was going to have on his once-orderly life. Oddly enough, the idea wasn't quite as disturbing as it might have been mere hours ago.

He glanced at his watch again, then scanned the crowd for a familiar head of short, reddish-brown hair. Sunny began to whimper, and he dug out the rubber teething ring Hetty had discovered under the cushion of the carrier. "Don't sweat it, sugar, we'll be home before you know it."

"Mercy, do you know what time it is?"

His head came up, and he frowned to cover his relief. She was back again, slipping through the fragile barricade with an air of having made it home safely.

"Time?"

"It's the middle of the night." She planted her back against the wall and lowered herself gracefully to the floor beside him. Her first act was to check on Sunny, which gave him a funny tight feeling in his throat. "It's crazy, isn't it? The way time loses all meaning? I can't even remember how long we've been here, much less—"

"How long until we get out," he finished for her.

She smiled, but the smile didn't quite reach her eyes. He wondered if she was finally going to lose her grip. He'd been waiting, expecting tears, complaints and the rest of the package to come pouring out. It had been his experience that women were quick to let the world know when things didn't go to suit them.

"I never saw so many fancy phones. When I finally

got to one I knew how to use, the office was closed. They have a twenty-four-hour, 800 line, but it stayed busy for so long I gave up.''

''Hardly surprising, under the circumstances. I figured you were having trouble getting through, you were away so long.''

He'd figured no such thing, but he wasn't going to admit it.

''Yes, well, like I said, there are so many kinds of phones now that I've never learned how to use, and then I got to talking to this nice woman who was traveling with her three teenage sons. They're from Omaha. Her husband's a cement contractor, and the boys are all planning to go into the family business as soon as they graduate from high school. I think that's real nice, don't you?''

What he thought was that it was highly irrelevant, and wondered where she'd been all her life that a simple pay phone was beyond her experience, but he refrained from saying so.

''I guess you think I'm ignorant—about the phones and all, but I told you I haven't traveled much.''

Sunny started to fuss. Hetty reached over and captured one of her tiny feet, cupping it in her hand. ''Did you wash the bottle after last time?''

''I did the best I could without soap. Damn, I hate this! What if she gets sick? What if her rash gets worse?''

''You simply climb on a chair and ask if there's a doctor in the house. At least that's the way it's done in the movies.''

"Yeah, right."

"Jax, don't worry so much. Most babies have a diaper rash at one time or another. We'll just have to keep her dry, that's all."

"What if she catches something? There are people from all over the world here—one of them might be carrying a germ or a virus."

Hetty couldn't help but be amused, even though she knew better than most how scary caring for a baby could be for an inexperienced parent. "She'll let you know if she's not feeling well."

"By crying. Right. Only, how'm I supposed to know if she's sick or just wet again? Or worse?"

"Worse, you'll know. Wet's pretty much a given. A lot of her fussiness is teething, though. She's got two tiny nubbins almost through, didn't her mama tell you?"

It wasn't the first time she'd referred obliquely to Carolyn. Jax had a feeling she was curious about why he was traveling alone with a baby he obviously didn't know a damned thing about. Luckily she seemed as disinclined as he was to discuss personal matters.

Which was just one more way in which she differed from the women he knew.

One bottle and two stale pimento sandwiches later, the weather picture hadn't improved. At last report, nothing was moving on land or in the air. Every airport east of the Mississippi between Nashville and New England was either iced in or fogged in. On one of the runways, a scraper had run into the wing of a

747, damaging both. Even after the weather cleared up, things were going to be in a hell of a mess until they sorted out the logistic tangles.

Hetty's head had once more settled on his shoulder, her soft breath purring warmly against his throat. Sunny was draped across her lap sleeping, fed, dried and burped. The burping was news to him. Carolyn had forgotten to mention it, but it seemed to make a difference. Whoever and whatever else Hetty Reynolds was, she was a godsend, given the circumstances.

He wondered if she had kids of her own. Where were they? Had she given them away? Dropped them off in a diner the way his mother had done him when he was six years old and then forgotten to come back for him for the next thirty-three years?

Jax blinked sleepily and considered easing them into a more comfortable position. Maybe later, he thought, his gaze on the hand that was resting protectively on Sunny's back.

No rings. Funny things, hands. They said a lot about a person. Hers weren't at all the kind of hands he would have expected on a woman whose traveling outfit consisted of slinky sweaters, long, flowered skirts and a subtle perfume that reminded him of summer nights in Virginia, a long, long time ago.

His stomach growled. His eyelids drooped. They'd all be a lot more comfortable lying down, with Sunny in her carrier between them, but if he woke her now, she'd go all self-conscious again.

Funny woman.

* * *

Nothing had changed when Hetty opened her eyes. Every bone and muscle in her body protested, and she blinked several times to clear her vision. The light hadn't changed. It could be noon or midnight. The crowd, if anything, was thicker, but at least it was quieter now. Exhausted travelers were sleeping wherever they could find a few clear feet of floor. Those who were lucky enough to have snared a seat were snoring, their heads either tipped back at an awkward angle or resting on their chests. One man had draped a newspaper over his face. Hetty stared, fascinated, as it lifted and fell, lifted and fell with each breath.

Only gradually did she become aware that she was lying on the floor on her side, with Jax's arm around her and Sunny sleeping peacefully in the carrier between him and the wall.

He stirred and mumbled something without waking up. The baby whimpered. Hetty thought, never in a million years would anyone believe this. Meeting a handsome stranger, sleeping with him on the floor of an airport? Surrounded by thousands of people, all going nowhere?

Uh-uh. This was like a play by that Kafka fellow. Surreal. Done in shades of gray, with no discernible plot, or at least, none she could follow.

Her eyes fuzzy with sleep, she tried and failed to focus on her watch. At this rate she was going to be cutting it awfully close. What if she didn't make it in time? What then?

It never occurred to her to feel sorry for herself.

Instead she thought, All that insurance money, wasted. I'm sorry, Gus.

She'd spent most of Gus's insurance, after his burial expenses, on his mother and daughter. Jeannie had a habit of running up bills that Hetty had paid, rather than see her rebellious stepdaughter get into any more trouble.

Jeannie's boyfriend, Nicky, had been a dreadful influence all through junior high, but nothing Hetty said had made a difference, and by then Sadie, Gus's mother, had suffered the first in a series of strokes. She'd been no help at all.

In the end, the young lovers had dropped out of school and run away. Eight months later Jeannie had come home long enough to leave her infant son. That had been five months ago.

"Here, now that I'm gone, you might as well have somebody else to boss around," she'd said. "Daddy and I were getting along just fine before you tricked him into marrying you."

Hetty let it pass. That hadn't been the way it was at all, but by then, she knew better than to argue. People heard what they wanted to hear, believed what they wanted to believe. For the next several months she'd had her hands too full to worry.

Robert had thrived. Sadie hadn't been able to help, but she'd been a wealth of information. They hadn't heard from Jeannie except indirectly. Someone had seen them in a bus station in Oklahoma City. Someone else said they were both working at a truck stop grill outside Tulsa.

Then Sadie died in her sleep. An embolism, according to her doctor. She had willed her car, which had sat up on blocks for years, to Hetty. She'd left her house to Jeannie. Hetty had finally located the girl, too late for her grandmother's funeral, but not too late for Jeannie and Nicky to claim the house, their son, and to inform Hetty that her services were no longer needed.

Which was when she'd impulsively decided to take what was left of the insurance money and blow it all on this trip and a wardrobe suitable for a romantic, once-in-a-lifetime cruise. Foolish?

Try stupid. Try silly, impractical, selfish and all the other things she'd tried so hard all her life not to be, because when he was drinking, which was most of the time, her father used to accuse her of being a dumb, selfish slut just like her mama.

Lying awake, she gradually became aware of her surroundings. Of the mingled smell of popcorn, stale chili, baby powder. The leathery, masculine smell of Jax's coat.

She tried not to think about all the what-ifs, but it was no good. They crowded in, anyway.

What if she missed the cruise? What if she wound up in Miami with no job, no friends, no place to stay and not enough money to get home again? Wherever home was.

What if Minco, Oklahoma, was only a figment of her imagination? What if the world began and ended right here in this madhouse of an airport?

"What if you just go to the bathroom, splash your

face with cold water and stop all this silliness,'' she muttered aloud.

Beside her, Jax stirred. He was spooned around her body, his right arm draped over her waist. Her mind might be racing like a hamster on a treadmill, but physically she felt incredibly safe.

Or maybe she didn't....

Against her back she could feel Jax's hard body shifting. He flung his free arm over his head. His knuckles struck the wall, and he mumbled a curse word.

Hetty didn't utter a sound. Did he realize she could feel what was happening to him? Was it...intentional, or was it just that thing that happened to men early in the morning?

Gus had found it embarrassing, but then, Jax was nothing at all like her late husband. She couldn't imagine Jax ever apologizing for being...well... aroused.

Hetty knew the instant he became aware of the situation, because he began to draw away from her. She wished she could sink through the floor, but as that was hardly likely, she tried to pretend she was just waking up.

Yawning and stretching, she wondered if her eyes were either puffy or shadowed or both. Both, probably. It was the way she reacted to lack of sleep. She'd never particularly worried about her lack of looks, but at this moment she'd have given everything she possessed to be beautiful. To have hair that wasn't flat on one side from being slept on and fuzzy everywhere else, thanks to some distant ancestor who was obviously related to a sheep.

She probably had finger marks on her cheek, too. Great.

"You awake?" Jax whispered. He'd shifted enough so that his arousal was no longer probing her backside. Either that or one look at her had cooled his early-morning ardor.

"About half-awake."

"Looks like nothing's changed."

"I don't see people rushing toward our gate. Maybe if we went around to the south side of the terminal, things would be different."

"This is the south side," Jax said wryly.

"Oh."

"You want to take a bathroom break first?"

"If you don't mind." She'd give her last five dollars for a toothbrush. Why hadn't her friendly travel agent warned her about things like this? She'd have stuck one in her purse.

"Toothpaste and shaving soap in my briefcase. You're welcome to anything you want."

Hetty sat up, raked her fingers through her hair and said, "Bless you! I'd have brought my own supplies in my purse if I'd thought about it."

He handed her a small tube of shaving soap, the old-fashioned kind that required a brush, and one of toothpaste. Hetty thought it was sweet. The only two men she'd known well enough to know their shaving habits used the stuff in an aerosol can.

"When you get back, I'll go and then reconnoiter

for supplies. Coffee and anything else I can find, right?''

They disentangled assorted limbs, straps, coats and shawls, and in the process Hetty was reminded all over again of just what an attractive man Jackson Powers was. Even rumpled, unshaven, his thick hair looking as if it had just been combed with a thresher.

And to think she'd slept with him.

Mercy!

Ten o'clock came and went. Hetty popped a cold, limp French fry into her mouth and wondered whether to call it breakfast, lunch or an early dinner. At this point she was no longer even sure what day it was. ''I've been thinking—what if this thing we call an airport is really a small planet circling in outer space? What if we're all alone in the universe?''

''Read a lot of science fiction, do you?''

''If the library has it, I've read it. Some of it's boring, but it's still another point of view. That's always—well, almost always—enlightening.''

''Interesting perspective.''

''I think so, too. That's why I've plowed through so many boring books.'' She checked the snap on her purse, then laid it aside. ''I tried the travel agency's 800 number again on the way from the rest room. It was still busy.''

''I'm not surprised,'' Jax said. He snagged the last French fry, wondering how long it was going to have to last. He'd had to search two different concourses before he'd found food this morning. Instead of coffee and pancakes, or anything else faintly resembling a breakfast, he'd had to settle for saltines, French fries and Bloody Mary mix. For ten bucks he'd managed to get a pint of whole milk for Sunny. He only hoped it didn't make her sick. Evidently formula had more ingredients than plain milk.

Hetty's shoulders were drooping. He told her to brace up, that things could be worse. Judging from the way her chin trembled, she wasn't far from tears.

God, he hoped she didn't start crying. When it came to dealing with feminine tears, he was at a dead loss, regardless of the age of the female.

She blew a wisp of hair off her forehead. "You reck'n?"

"I reck'n," he said, amused by the colloquialism.

"You're right. We could've been diverted to Alaska and had to make connections by dog sled."

"Or we could be in the air in all this mess. Or one of those poor devils trapped out on the runway. Given a choice, where would you rather be?"

He was trying to cheer her up, and Hetty appreciated it, she really did, only there was nothing cheerful in knowing that the one time in your life you did something truly frivolous, it turned out to be a monumental flop.

"You're a nice man, Jackson Powers." She managed a smile, despite the fact that she was probably going to miss her cruise. In spite of the fact that she was practically broke, with no job and no home to return to until she patched things up with Jeannie.

Which meant dealing with Nicky. Jeannie's new

husband recognized a good thing when it fell into his lap and wasn't about to let his stepmother-in-law horn in on it.

"How many cans of formula do we have left?" Jax asked briskly, as if knowing she could use a distraction.

"We're out. It'll have to be the milk next time. It might give her diarrhea, which could be a problem unless we can locate a source of diapers."

Hetty welcomed the chance to take on someone else's problems. Jax and Sunny weren't family, only passing strangers, but anything was better than being all alone in the wilderness of an overcrowded, shutdown airport with roughly a zillion frustrated holiday travelers.

You'd think she'd know more about airports, having been married to a pilot, but after years of selling hardware, Gus had barely gotten started on his cropdusting career before he'd been killed.

"Want to go check out the weather report again?" Jax asked. He had the most remarkable eyes. Hetty couldn't decide whether they were charcoal-gray or navy-blue. Mostly he kept his feelings hidden, but she'd caught glimpses of humor and concern. Once or twice she'd seen something that looked almost like admiration.

Which had to be wishful thinking on her part.

"Can we afford to leave our space unguarded?" Miracle of miracles, no one had tried to push past their fragile barrier. Jax had moved a sign advertising a Bermuda Cruise so that it hid the area where they'd slept.

"There's a lot of coughing and sneezing going on. I don't mind taking my chances, but I hate to expose Sunny any more than I have to."

It was decided that they would take turns scouting out food and information, and baby-sitting. He said, "I'll make a run and see if I can round up some diapers and baby food."

"I think I saw a drugstore down that way about half a mile," Hetty offered.

There had to be something in an airport this size. It was almost a small city in itself. "I'll give it a shot," he said as he eased past the wheelchair.

She smiled, and without realizing it, Jax smiled back and went on smiling for the next few minutes until he caught himself at it.

He wasn't a smiler. It wasn't his nature. Something—either the ice storm or the woman—was royally screwing him up.

The day passed in slow motion, as if the hands of all the clocks had gone on strike. From sheer boredom, they lapsed into a desultory conversation. It started when Hetty caught him looking at her hands. She had polished her nails for the first time in years, but no amount of polish could disguise years of housework, minus all but the most basic appliances.

"I told you I'd been married. I don't wear my wedding ring because it makes my fingers break out," she confided diffidently.

"You're divorced?" He knew several divorced women who had shifted their rings to the other hand. It was a personal choice, he supposed.

"My husband died."

"Oh. Sorry." He told her his secretary was allergic to anything that contained fragrance, but not to metal.

"My mother-in-law was allergic to animals. She used to live on a farm, too."

Jax murmured a polite response, and Hetty went on to describe the house and the barn that had been turned into a hangar, where Gus had kept his green-and-yellow Cessna.

She told him about the potholders her mother-in-law had made. "She must have crocheted five hundred of the things before her last stroke. She couldn't get out of bed, but she had the use of her hands right up until the last few months. I think it helped, having something to do."

"Your husband was a pilot?"

"A crop duster. That is, he was a helicopter pilot during the Vietnam War. For a while he didn't want to fly at all, but then this plane went up for sale and he got interested again, and one thing led to another."

Jax studied her for a long moment, making her aware all over again of how awful she must look. Something, probably the dry air, was making her hair frizz up all over her head. Not even the best haircut could change that, although even Jeannie, who'd barely been speaking to her by then, had agreed the cut was an improvement.

"A 'Nam vet, hmm? He must've been a few years older than you."

"Age is irrelevant. Gus was the dearest man in the world. I've never known him to raise his voice, much less his hand, to anyone, no matter what the provocation."

Gradually Jax drew forth her story. He wasn't a trial lawyer, but he did know how to elicit information. He also knew how to read between the lines. Either she was a damned good liar or he was going to have to realign his thinking when it came to women. Hetty Reynolds didn't fit any recognizable pattern.

Under the circumstances he couldn't very well walk off and leave her to fend for herself, but he hoped to hell the weather broke before he got in any deeper.

Three

———

Stress. His doctor had told him four years ago, when he'd gone in for his last annual physical, that stress was a silent killer. Since then Jax had concentrated on relaxing whenever he could find time. It worked pretty well as long as nothing happened to blow his orderly routine, which could accommodate any number of international maritime disputes, ship disasters, oil spills and the like.

It was what happened outside his professional life that tended to screw up the works. A couple of impulsive acts and his whole life had suddenly lost steerage. Impulse one had been buying an old relic of a schooner last fall. For nearly a century the *Lizzie-Linda* had worked the waterways from Maryland to

North Carolina, first as an oyster boat, then as a freighter. There wasn't a lick of paint left on her anywhere. Five inches of her eight-inch log bottom were rotten, yet something about her graceful lines and proud bearing had struck an unsuspected lode of romanticism buried deep inside him. For the cost of hauling and back storage he'd bought her and eventually found a place where he could keep her. Since then he'd spent most of his spare time and a considerable portion of his funds trying to patch her up.

Impulse two had been Carolyn. About eighteen months ago he'd spent a week on the West Coast combining business with pleasure.

Enter Sunny. She of the soggy bottom, the toothless grins and those big, navy-blue eyes that had drilled straight through his defenses the first time he'd seen her.

Talk about your impulses!

As if that weren't enough, he had to hook up with a woman who didn't fit into any of his neat pigeonholes. A woman with eyes the color of rainwater and a body like a walking wet dream. A woman who spoke softly and sang husky, off-key lullabies to a stranger's crying baby.

A woman who curled up on a hard floor and trustingly thrust her backside into his groin.

Jax swore silently, pried open the tin of aspirin, chased a couple with a shot from the water fountain and chewed on another antacid tablet. He was no health nut, but all the same, he hoped nobody in this mob was carrying any exotic, multiresistant bugs.

With all the coughing and sneezing going on all around them, Sunny could easily catch something.

"Any news?" Tucking the blanket around the sleeping baby, he watched Hetty slip back through the narrow opening. Her skirt snagged on the Bermuda Cruise sign, pulling taut against her neat little behind for a moment. He tried unsuccessfully not to notice.

Stress. It made a man do crazy things, all right. Even scarier, it made him think crazy thoughts.

"I stopped to watch a weather update on TV. You wouldn't believe what's going on," she said breathlessly. "Tornadoes in Tennessee and Arkansas, floods in the northwest and an avalanche somewhere in France. I heard some people a few gates down talking about the apocalypse. One woman kept insisting it was a natural cycle and that contrary to popular belief we're simply entering another glacial age."

"In that case, I guess we might as well settle down for the next few millennia."

She nodded with mock gravity. "In other words, this is going to be another tomb, like the pyramids or one of those ancient garbage dumps archeologists are always discovering, full of pots and old bones and arrowheads. Is that what you're saying?"

"I think they're called kitchen middens."

"Not this one. All the food stands have closed. They're saying nobody showed up for work today and, anyway, they can't get fresh supplies in."

"Hardly surprising." Jax was distracted by the way her hair slid across her cheeks as she settled beside him. He was no expert, but the color, as near as he could place it, was somewhere between heart cedar and red oak. More red than brown, with golden glints.

She sighed, loosened the light blanket Jax had just tucked tightly around Sunny's feet and said, "What do you suppose an archeologist would think if a thousand years from now he came across all this?" She waved her hands expressively. "All of us here and our luggage, all tangled up with rusted airplanes and whatever's left of the buildings?"

"That some of us probably starved to death and others succumbed because they didn't know how to dress for the weather," Jax said dryly. "Here, put this on." He handed her his jacket.

"Are you sure?"

She reminded him of a gray-eyed doe, which made about as much sense as anything else that had trudged through his mind lately. "Yeah, I'm fine. Warm-natured. You're starting to shiver."

"It feels like there's a draft, but it might be because I'm cold-natured."

"Right. That explains why you're dressed in summer clothes in the middle of an ice storm."

"I told you, I was supposed to go to Florida. I'd have looked silly boarding a cruise liner in my winter coat and woolies."

He let it pass. Under the circumstances it was a wonder they weren't at each other's throats. People tended to take out their frustrations on those closest, bickering for no good reason at all. He'd seen a fist fight break out a few hours ago over a week-old *Wall Street Journal*.

"The muscles at the back of my neck keep tightening up. Do you suppose it's from sleeping on the floor?" she asked.

"Relax. Flex your shoulders. Better still, turn around."

She turned, and he cupped his hands over the delicate bones of her shoulders and began to work his fingers against the tense muscles. She groaned. "Ahh, that feels wonderful," she murmured. "It hurts, but in a nice way."

His thumbs moved up under her hair. Her skin was soft and cool, her hair warm and silky. He had a sudden urge to place his mouth where his fingers were, and it scared him so much he dropped his hands, brushed them together and said briskly, "There, that ought to do it."

She sighed and slumped back against the wall. Jax sighed, too. He wasn't given to sighing. If he'd brought along his laptop he could've made some headway on the *Arzan* case, but he'd figured on a turnaround trip.

No more touching, he decided. Rationality was one of the first casualties in extraordinary circumstances. He'd read about a couple of strangers who'd been stuck in an elevator together for five hours. The guy had subsequently proposed, the woman accepted and the marriage had lasted all of three weeks.

For the next few hours Jax made a deliberate effort to avoid touching her. It only made things worse. Naturally his brain stayed focused on what it was he wasn't supposed to do.

She had to be as aware of the growing tension as he was. The more they avoided even the slightest accidental touch, the more some mysterious magnetic force attracted his hand to her shoulder, her hand to his arm. Both pairs of eyes to both pairs of lips.

Dammit, they were strangers, Jax reminded himself. Ships that pass in the endless foggy, sleety, icebound night.

With no breakfast, lunch or dinner to divide the time into measurable segments, they took brief naps, then woke to go check and see if anything had changed.

Nothing had. Gates were unmanned. Information stations were swamped. The official line was that weather improvements were expected momentarily. A warm front was moving up from the Gulf. Announcements would be made.

Sunny was handling things remarkably well, Hetty thought, for a teething baby with a diaper rash who stayed wet and hungry most of the time. She was learning to sit up. Robert, her stepgrandson, had sat alone at five months, but Hetty tactfully refrained from crowing. Sunny was heavier. Heavier babies had more to support.

Besides, she had a feeling Sunny had spent far more time in her carrier than Robert ever had.

For long stretches of time they remained silent. Oddly enough, it was a comfortable silence, yet awareness of each other was never far from the surface.

Jax wondered how long she'd been widowed and if she'd taken a lover yet. He wondered what her husband had been like and how good their marriage had been. There'd been a considerable age difference, if the guy was a 'Nam vet.

Hetty wondered about Sunny's mother, and what had happened between the two of them. She wondered about the other women in his life. Surely there must be someone. Jax wasn't the kind of man not to be romantically involved. He practically radiated sex appeal.

Only not with her. Not intentionally, at least. Not that she expected him to make a pass, because even with her new clothes and her new hairstyle, she was still plain old Hetty Reynolds.

Bored, restless, frustrated and physically uncomfortable, they lapsed into small talk to pass the time. It wasn't something Jax excelled in, but it beat dwelling on all the work piling up on his desk. Not that he was obsessed by his profession, but when a man contracted to do something, he was obligated to follow through. It was a creed he'd learned early and had done his best ever since to live up to.

Hetty sighed and shifted her position. ''This floor's not getting any softer.'' Beyond the glaring lights outside, the sky was dark.

It was as close as she'd come to a complaint. Jax wished he had a cushion to offer her, but his coat was covering Sunny now that her blankets had to double as diapers. He could offer his lap, but under the circumstances, that probably wouldn't be smart.

"So, d'you want to talk politics?" he asked after another long stretch of silence. "How about religion? Favorite foods? Nah, scratch that." He dug out his roll of antacid tablets, offered her one and when she declined, absently popped one in his mouth to offset the effect of aspirin on his stomach lining.

"Your head still hurts, doesn't it?"

He nodded, then wished he hadn't. "Not bad. Probably low barometric pressure."

"Or noise. Or lack of a decent meal. Or all this awful uncertainty. I hate uncertainty, don't you?"

"Nothing's ever certain." He shrugged, then confessed. "Yeah, I do. Too much, I guess. I've always been subject to rules. Boarding school, marine corps, law school." He wasn't into confidences, but hell…ships that pass in the night, and all that.

"I guess rules are sort of like a tight girdle. While it might be miserable, at least it smooths out the bulges and you know you're not jiggling."

He lifted both eyebrows, his gaze moving slowly down her wand-slender form. "You're kidding."

"Not me—I mean, I don't wear a girdle—oh, mercy, I don't believe I said that. Honestly, I'm not in the habit of discussing my underwear with strange men."

"I'm not all that strange," he said with a crooked grin.

"No, you're not," she said earnestly. "Jax, I really don't know how to thank you for—well, for taking me under your wing. I might've mentioned before that I'm not really a very experienced traveler. I'd probably have panicked.''

"No, you wouldn't. I suspect Hetty Reynolds is a lot stronger than she pretends." He studied her intently for a moment before his gaze softened, straying to her mouth to linger there before returning to her eyes again. Her lips, naked and vulnerable, trembled once, then firmed, and he thought, yeah, you're a lot stronger than you look, lady.

He couldn't help but wonder what had made her that way.

The food machines were still empty. No surprise. The concessions were still closed in all the terminals, also no great surprise. Sunny drank the last of the whole milk diluted with bottled water and chewed frantically on her teething ring, then fussed herself to sleep while Hetty crooned a husky, off-key lullaby about looking glasses and mockingbirds.

And because her voice affected him in a totally inappropriate way, Jax took a jog on the moving sidewalk. To loosen up his muscles, he'd explained, telling her he'd be back in twenty minutes.

He returned in thirty-five with a half-melted candy bar. He'd paid a kid twenty bucks for the thing, then felt guilty for depriving a growing boy of sustenance.

Sunny was sleeping soundly, undisturbed by the constant din all around them. "Here, I got lucky," he said, tossing the candy bar to Hetty.

"Oh, wonderful!" And then she lifted stricken eyes to his. "But what about you? I'll break it in half—wait a minute, maybe I can cut it with—'' She rummaged in her big, lumpy shoulder bag.

"I already ate mine. Sorry. I didn't think you'd mind."

There'd been only one. He was so hungry his belly was knotted around his backbone, yet he took great satisfaction in being able to provide for his unexpected family. He'd found a new source of bottled water, also at a price, and stocked up. Two liters. That should last for the duration. Something had to break loose pretty soon.

"Oh, mmm, this is scrumptious!"

Jax tucked his coat around Sunny's feet. They had two thin flannel blankets left to use as diapers. Hetty had tried washing them, but with no soap and no place to dry them, it wasn't a very satisfactory arrangement. Things had to start moving pretty soon. He'd never heard of a delay this long.

Now and then someone would approach the impromptu barrier he'd erected and linger, as if sizing up his chance of claiming a few feet of the space they'd commandeered, then shrug and move on. Jax slid down beside her. Feeling protective, he sat closer than absolutely necessary. Funny the way a minor disaster could turn a civilized maritime lawyer into a caveman. If anyone actually tried to horn in, what would he do? Use his briefcase as a club? Resort to fists?

There'd been a time when fists had served him well enough, during his early attempts to prove something to himself, before he'd learned that there were better ways.

"Hey, you're wasting chocolate," he murmured, lifting a thumb to her mouth. "Right...here." He wiped it off, his touch lingering longer than the task required, then licked his thumb.

She stared at him, eyes wide and startled. He was tempted to—

No he wasn't. He hadn't completely lost his mind. Not yet. "Know any good knock-knock jokes?" he asked a little desperately.

Her lips parted, revealing the chipped tooth that made her smile so oddly engaging. "Um, I can't think of any right now."

"How about puns? Or limericks?"

"None I could repeat in mixed company."

Quaint, he thought. He didn't know there was such a thing as mixed company these days. Tugging at the collar of his shirt, he said, "Whew, is it me, or is it getting warmer in here?"

"It's you. You're warm-natured, I'm cold-natured, remember? What if they run out of heating oil?"

"Heating oil?"

"For the furnaces."

Welcoming the distraction, Jax launched into a description of various climate control methods, which was perhaps more technical than necessary. Still, it served to get his mind back in line. For a minute there he'd been afraid he was going to embarrass himself.

Rumors flew. To their credit the airlines tried to get the word out. Trouble was, the word wasn't sufficient.

Nor was it encouraging. There was no longer even a pretense of going forth in search of food. Jax had managed to secure a supply of saltines for Sunny, but all the available airline caterers' meals had been wiped out in the first twenty-four hours, with no more coming in. Personal caches had long since been devoured in private or sold at a high profit. Even the supplies of peanuts and pretzels had been exhausted. If there was food to be had in the various private clubs, it was a well-kept secret. Jax suspected that those supplies, too, had run out like all the rest.

Hetty's stomach growled. "I can't believe this is happening in this day and age, in a civilized city like Chicago. You would think someone would do something," she grumbled softly. "For the children, at least. Sorry. I didn't mean to whine."

"Take my shaving soap and go wash your hands and face, you'll feel better. Jog for five minutes to loosen up. If you're not back by—" he glanced at his watch "—eleven-fifteen, Sunny and I'll come looking for you."

Doing anything was better than doing nothing. Besides, Hetty liked the smell of his shaving soap. It kept her from feeling quite so grungy. There were no amenities and little privacy in the rest room, but she did the best she could and then tried jogging.

She gave it up after the first few minutes. Long skirts and big-heeled sandals weren't made for it. She'd bought them only because she thought they were fashionable. Jeannie had delighted in telling her after she'd spent all her money that by the time anything made it to the discount stores, it was way out of style.

Not until she returned to drop, winded, onto the floor beside Jax and his daughter did she realize that something was missing.

"Oh, shoot, I must've left it in the rest room," she muttered.

"Left what?" Jax handed Sunny her teething ring again. She'd exhausted her supply of teething biscuits and was subsisting on water. Not liking it much, either.

"My purse. I know I had it when—" She struggled to get up again.

"Hetty, hold on, think this through before you go racing off in a blind panic."

"I'm not in a blind panic. I simply have to retrace my steps and find the thing. It's got my money, my tickets and hotel reservation number and everything in it. Without it, I'm— Oh, mercy, I've got to find it!"

Jax swore softly. Could any woman really be that naive? She had about as much chance of finding her purse in this mob as he did of sprouting wings and flying out of here. "Sit down, honey, let me round up someone from security. I wouldn't count on getting it back, though."

"That woman I was telling you about? The one whose husband is a cement contractor, and whose three teenage sons are traveling with her? She might've seen something. I was talking to her outside the rest room. She was showing me some pictures of her cat, and I was showing her pictures of Robert—I told you about Robert, didn't I?''

Not only told him, she'd shown him the pictures. Her family, such as it was—all steps and in-laws— seemed to mean a lot to her.

He figured the friendly old woman and her equally friendly sons—if they really were her sons—might have had a small scam going. God knows it wouldn't be the first time some lowlife had taken advantage of a disaster. Looters seemed to crawl out of the woodwork after every catastrophe, big or small.

Finding any uniformed personnel was next to impossible. Whenever any one of them, from the cleaning crew on up, showed their faces, they were mobbed. Nevertheless Jax finally managed to talk to someone from security, only to be told that one missing purse was far down on the priority list. In this terminal alone they had nine missing children, three women in labor at last count, two heart attacks and a diplomat with two broken fingers.

On hearing what he had to report, Hetty swallowed hard. He wondered if she was going to cry. Two crying females might be more than he could handle at one time.

She fooled him. Took a deep, shuddering breath and said, ''Thanks for trying. I really do appreciate it, because I wouldn't even know where to start.''

Her chin wobbled once before she got it under control. But when the tip of her nose got suspiciously red, Jax simply opened his arms. After only a brief hesitation, she walked into them, lowered her head to his shoulder and opened the floodgates.

"Go ahead, cry if it'll make you feel better," he offered generously.

"It w-won't. It'll only make m-my throat ache."

But she cried, and he held her because it was the right thing to do. And because he damned well wanted to hold her! He didn't know how much she'd been carrying in her purse—a few traveler's checks, her tickets and baggage claims, probably, along with the kind of things most women carried in purses. Family photos, credit cards, makeup...

He could help her with the financial stuff once he got past her prickly pride, but at the moment he had other things on his mind. He'd meant only to comfort her in her loss. Unfortunately *comfort* didn't begin to describe the feelings that coursed through his body. As her warm tears soaked through his shirt, he was aware of a growing warmth in another region. It didn't help matters at all.

Leaning against the wall, he held her until the shudders subsided, and then he patted her back clumsily, all the while trying to ease her body away from his.

It wasn't working. "Feeling better now?" he asked, forcing a false note of cheeriness.

"Don't look at me, I'm all red-eyed and awful looking."

"Yeah, you're a monster, all right." He dug out

his handkerchief, glanced at it and shoved it back into his pocket.

She took a deep gulp of air and lifted her face from his shoulder, but made no attempt to disengage herself from his embrace. "I'm all right now."

Jax gave up. She had to be aware of what was happening to him. There was no way he could disguise his arousal, but it was damned poor timing, considering the fact that they were in a public place, surrounded by hundreds, if not thousands, of people.

Because he couldn't seem to help himself, his hand slid down to her hips, pressing her tightly against him. It only made things worse. Her mouth was mere inches from his, her eyes closed, the lashes glistening with tears.

Well, what the hell—he was only human.

The kiss began tentatively. Warm, hard lips brushed against soft, moist ones. Within seconds it turned into something altogether different. Something wild, demanding. Something dangerous.

Jax twisted his head for better contact, at the same time thrusting against her in a way that was unmistakably carnal. Heart racing, hands trembling, he was torn between the temptation to cover her firm bottom with both hands and grind her groin against his, and the equally strong temptation to fill both his hands with her breasts.

He tasted her tears, thought how fragile she felt in his arms, how incredibly desirable. How much he would like to lay her on the floor, uncover her treasures one by one and bury himself in her feminine depths.

Trouble, Powers. Better back off while you still can. Remember that pair in the elevator?

Nice try, but it wasn't working. He broke away, muttered an apology, then quickly found her mouth again. She was like a hungry bird, open and waiting for him.

In the end it was Hetty whose good sense prevailed. She turned her head, gasping to catch her breath. "We can't—I shouldn't—you don't—"

Leaning his forehead against hers, he laughed harshly and said, "All of the above." He might have released her then, but for the embarrassingly obvious bulge in the front of his flannels.

It was Hetty who took the initiative by stepping away. "I don't know what happened," she said with all the dignity she could muster, considering she'd been ready a minute before to lie down and take a stranger into her body.

She waited. She had her flaws, every one of which she'd been recently reminded of by her stepson-in-law. But dishonesty wasn't among them, so she added, "Well, that's not really true."

Jax turned his back to her, braced one arm against the wall, then leaned his forehead against it. She stared at his back, wanting to touch him again—needing the warmth and strength he possessed. Feeling awkward, she wondered if he was as embarrassed as she was by what had just happened. For a woman who'd been married as long as she had—a grandmother, for heaven's sake—she was behaving like a teenager.

Worse. Jeannie had known more about such things at fourteen than Hetty did at thirty-seven.

"Well, I don't know about you, but I could do with a drink of water," she said brightly.

He made a sound that defied interpretation just as the loudspeaker crackled and a voice came on with an announcement.

Four

Excitement hummed throughout the giant airport, its terminals flung out like the tentacles of an octopus. Finally things were beginning to move! A fleet of scrapers was fanning out toward the runways. The cold front had moved out over the Atlantic; Norfolk and Atlanta would be up and running within the hour. Further bulletins would be issued as flights were rescheduled.

The announcement could be heard echoing throughout the terminal, accompanied by tired cheers as people began gathering up their possessions.

Not Hetty. She had nothing to gather. She had searched the bathroom for her purse and Jax had checked with security again, as well as lost and found.

"Well," she said decisively. Forcing a smile, she fought back the panic that threatened to overcome her again.

Dear Lord, what was she going to do? Traveler's aid? She'd seen a sign about halfway down the corridor, but the crowd around it had been so thick, she hadn't even attempted to get through.

Besides, what could they do? Offer condolences? They certainly weren't going to offer her money, which was what she needed. If they handed out loans to every fly-by-night stranger who asked, they'd be out of business in no time.

She was going to have to call her friend at the agency. The 800 number had been busy every time she'd tried, but sooner or later she was bound to get through. If not, she would have to reverse the charges and call her stepdaughter.

But what if Jeannie wasn't there? What if she was there, but hung up as soon as she heard Hetty's voice? Hetty fully intended to reclaim her family, but it was going to take time and patience. Asking for a loan was hardly the best way to begin.

Take a deep breath, Henrietta. Now, think. Would Oklahoma have an embassy in Illinois?

Probably not.

For a while adrenaline had carried her, but now that relief was finally within sight, exhaustion was rapidly setting in.

Jax, who'd been pacing the floor with Sunny on his shoulder, paused in front of where she was seated, both arms wrapped around her knees.

"How much baggage did you check?"

"Two bags. My iron and coffeemaker are in one, along with some books I've been wanting to read but haven't had time. I thought I'd have plenty of time on a cruise."

What she'd actually thought was that if she wasn't too busy partying with the kind of people who posed for the pictures on the brochure, she would head for the row of poolside lounge chairs, also pictured in the brochure, and catch up on her reading. She'd bought dark glasses, a wide-brimmed straw hat decorated with a big, yellow flower and a tropical-print bathing suit and cover-up, just for the occasion.

"When things calm down, I'll go with you to the baggage agent and see if we can reestablish your claim. You'll have to describe the bags and what's in them. You did have visible identification, didn't you?"

She assured him that the bags were clearly marked with her name, but no address. She'd read that in a travel magazine somewhere. Not to put your address on your luggage, because then anyone who happened to see it would know you weren't at home and could go to your address and break and enter at will.

Although in her case, it hardly applied. She no longer had a home.

"Watch the monitors. They're beginning to reschedule a few flights." Jax settled a drowsy and tear-stained Sunny in her carrier and sat down beside her.

Hetty squinted up over the heads of the crowd at the sign listing arrivals and departures by number and destination. Most were still designated as cancelled or delayed. ''Is your flight listed yet?'' She couldn't bear the thought that he would go first, leaving her behind.

''Not yet.''

At least on the planes they would have those tiny bars of soap, she thought. Despite two and a half days with only the most cursory washup, Jax still smelled of shaving soap and leather. Heaven only knew what she smelled like. Baby spit, probably.

''There goes another one to Orlando. It looks like things are beginning to get cracking. With Orlando open, Miami won't be a problem. You ought to be—'' Lowering his head to his knees, he swore softly. ''Dammit, I keep forgetting. Look, tell me what I can do to help. I'll buy you a ticket to wherever you need to go, although I can't do much about your cruise. I know the line—it's got a pretty good reputation, but I doubt if they'll return to port to collect one passenger. Do you have insurance? Credit cards usually offer some kind of protection. You can probably catch up with your ship at the next port of call.''

Jax watched as pride battled to overcome the terror of uncertainty. As bedraggled as she looked, that familiar cloak of dignity came over her again, touching him in a totally unexpected way.

''Actually, I didn't use a credit card, but I'll be just fine, really. I have friends—family. My friend at the travel agency will know what to do once I get through to her. I'll be just fine,'' she repeated in an obvious effort to convince herself.

''Yeah, sure you will. I just thought since you've

been such a great help, Sunny and I could repay the favor.''

The air between them grew distinctly cooler. ''Thank you,'' she said quietly, ''but I can manage quite well by myself. I told you I have—'' Abruptly, she started to rise and cried, ''Oh, darn!'' at the sound of tearing fabric.

''Sit down, Hetty.''

Defeated, she sat and examined the tear near the hem of her skirt. ''I stepped on my blasted skirt tail. I don't suppose you have a safety pin or any kind of tape?''

''No pin, no tape, not even a paper clip. Look, there's no point in wading into that traffic jam yet. Wherever you plan on going, you won't be boarding anytime soon. We need to talk.''

Hetty, trying not to think beyond the moment, said dully, ''There's no one at the desk yet, anyway. I don't even know if my flight will still be leaving from this gate. They might've changed everything around.'' It was no longer ''her flight,'' but there was nothing to be gained from belaboring the point. They'd been booked on different flights, both with the same small airline. The only reason they had met at all was that both flights had been posted at the same desk.

Hetty's thoughts veered off on a path best left unexplored. She couldn't imagine being in the same airport with Jax Powers and not knowing it. Could a magnet ignore the presence of iron?

No more than she could ignore the physical attraction she felt for this one man. And the scariest part of all was that it wasn't entirely physical.

Correction: the scariest part was that he would be leaving her all too soon, and that would be the end of it.

Whatever *it* was.

Jax knew she was worried sick. He wanted to place a reassuring arm around her shoulder, but didn't dare. Not when even the most casual touch could escalate to full-fledged arousal. Which, under the circumstances, was not only ludicrous, it was dangerous.

He cleared his throat. "Keep watching the board. Once my flight's posted, I'll get in line at the desk. Meanwhile, neither of us is going anywhere for a while, so we might as well sit tight."

He cleared his throat and frowned, wondering how to phrase the idea that had been taking shape in his mind for the past few hours. "Look, Hetty, I've got a proposition for you."

Eyeing him warily, she tucked her skirt tightly around her ankles and edged away. Dammit, he hadn't meant to spook her, but if she was too proud to take his money he was going to have to come up with another way to help her. He had a pretty good idea from a few things she'd let drop that her family wasn't going to come through for her. Nor did he hold out much hope of contacting her travel agency until things settled down. This was more than a local problem. The whole country was affected in one way or another.

But there was no way he was going to walk away

when his flight was called, leaving her here all alone. "Next time you might consider electronic ticketing," he said dryly, and then had to explain what it was. His expression must have given him away, because she immediately turned defensive.

"I might not know all there is to know about a few of the newer technological gadgets, but I do have a microwave. I have a VCR. I even know how to program it."

"Congratulations, I can still screw up on that."

"I seriously doubt that."

"Hey, I'm good but I'm not perfect," he confessed, hoping to lure a smile from behind the shadows. He considered telling her about the *Lizzie-Linda* and his one crazy attempt to get in touch with his roots.

And then he reconsidered.

Silently they watched the board and waited for their flights to be posted. Hetty had thought things through and come up with a plan. She would wait until the crowd thinned out and then find someone in authority. If she explained about her stolen purse, and how it wouldn't have happened if her flight hadn't been cancelled, then she might eventually get a free flight back to Oklahoma City.

She would demand it. She might not look it in her fancy cruise wear, but she was tough as ironwood. She'd faced adversity of one kind or another all her life without buckling under. It might take a few hours, or even another day, but if she persisted, sooner or later she would win. It was only fair.

But just in case, she'd better hedge her bets, as her father would've said.

She cleared her throat. "I'm not sure what you had in mind, but I might consider accepting a small loan if you'll give me your address so I can pay you back when I get settled."

Jax tried and failed to suppress a grin. Even begging, the lady had class. "Consider it done."

"Yes, well, first I thought I might try the phone again. If I still can't get through to the agency, I'll call Jeannie. My stepdaughter? I told you about her, didn't I?"

She had. And about her husband, the late, great Gus, who had never raised his voice to her, much less a hand. A statement which had given rise to more questions than he cared to ask, or she would've cared to answer.

"Sure, no problem. You can use my calling card. There's still too much interference for my cell phone to work."

"Calling cards are like credit cards, right?"

"Pretty much."

"Then, no thank you, I'll borrow some change instead if you don't mind."

Jax dug out a handful of pocket change and added a few bills. "You do know how to use a change machine?"

"I do know how to use a change machine," she assured him. "I can also change a tire and change the oil in a pickup truck, as long as it's not one of the newer models."

She tried for a haughty look, but the corner of her mouth was twitching. Scared or not, the lady had guts. And style. And class. The combination of too much pride and too little sophistication could be tough to handle, but he'd bet on her to come through this thing with flying colors.

Especially if she went along with what he had to propose.

"You're sure I have time? Will you watch the board while I'm gone?"

"Like a hawk. So far, the earliest flight scheduled to Atlanta is early afternoon." He glanced at his watch. "It's not even noon. No need to hurry."

Under several silky layers of knit, garnished by the bedraggled, well-chewed shawl, her shoulders squared. "I'm sure I can get on a flight back home if I explain things. Maybe not right away, but—do you suppose there'll be food on board?"

Ah, geez. He knew for a fact that all she'd had in the past twenty-four hours was water and a candy bar. Not a word of complaint, though. She had grit, he'd hand her that. Not for the first time he wondered about the woman who wore impractical, summer clothes in the middle of a winter storm, as if she'd stepped out of the pages of a travel magazine. The woman with the guileless eyes and the seductive walk. The woman who couldn't carry a tune in a bucket, but who could lull a fussy baby to sleep—and incidentally turn a man on—with a husky, off-key lullaby.

He thought of the two women who'd had the greatest impact on his own life. Each of them had given away their own child. Breaking off the unproductive line of thought, he said, ''While you're out there, see if any of the other desks have opened up yet. I'll keep an eye on ours.''

His eyes remained on the nearby vacant console, but his mind was busy trying to come up with a way of getting Hetty booked on his own flight. There was no reason for her to go to Miami now; she'd missed too much of her cruise. Without her luggage, the rest wouldn't be much fun. He had a feeling there was no real reason for her to go back to Oklahoma, either.

On the other hand, he'd hate to get her hopes up prematurely. One way or another he intended to pull it off, but it might be tricky with all the conflicting demands.

He'd been staring in the direction in which she'd disappeared for nearly ten minutes before he realized what he was doing. Swearing softly, he reached over the row of seats that formed one of the barriers and scooped up a discarded newspaper. It was three days old, but it might serve to get his mind back on track.

He was actually dozing when she returned. Sensing her presence, he opened his eyes and stared up at her, seeing a beautiful woman in dirty, wrinkled clothes. A woman with shadows under her eyes, a tired droop to her mouth and a look of…what, compassion?

Well, hell.

''You're exhausted. You were sleeping so soundly I hated to wake you up.''

Not a word about his not watching the monitors. He'd almost rather she chewed him out. "Any luck?"

She shook her head, braced her back against the wall and slid down beside him, drawing her knees up close to her body. "I finally got through to the agency, but wouldn't you know it? My friend's been out with the flu. The woman who answered was just filling in. She sounded as if she weren't at all sure what she was doing. Anyway, she promised to call the airline and see if she can't get me home again."

Along with a few hundred thousand others, he thought, but said nothing. He didn't have to. "I called Jeannie next. Nicky answered. He's Jeannie's husband. We don't really get along too well, and when I told him who I was, he said Jeannie was out and he was busy, and he hung up." She sighed. "Here's the rest of your change."

He took it. She had her pride. At the moment it was about all she did have.

Purely as a diversion, he launched into a fresh topic of conversation. "Did I ever tell you about my great-great-grandfather?"

"Your what?" She stared at him as if he'd finally cracked.

"My father's side of the family. I'd never heard about him until I was fifteen, and haven't spent much time thinking about him since. But after Sunny's appearance on the scene, I've been struck by an odd coincidence."

If he'd wanted to distract her, to break through that

tricky combination of pride, panic and vulnerability, he'd succeeded.

"What coincidence?" she asked suspiciously. "Where does Sunny fit into your great-great-grandfather's coincidence?"

"First you have to know that I was adopted at age six by an elderly relative after my mother dropped out of sight. I never heard from her again until one day, out of the blue, I got this package in the mail from a law firm in Missouri. My mother had died, and among her things was a bundle of letters from my dad, written when he was in Korea. I think they must have separated before he went. Years later I learned that he'd been killed there, but that's not the story I set out to tell."

Hetty ached for the child who had grown up without a father and whose mother had abandoned him without a backward look. At least she had memories, even though not all of them were good.

"There was a diary—more of a log book, actually—that had been packed away all these years along with my father's things. Thank God my mother didn't toss it all out, the way she did—"

He broke off, and Hetty wondered what all this had to do with anything. Wondered even more why he was telling her now, just as they were about to go their separate ways. They'd talked about everything under the sun just to pass the time, but nothing really personal.

Well, she might have mentioned something about her own family. After all, what else did she have to talk about? But now that he was about to leave, she didn't really want to know about his family. He was going to be hard enough to forget without being able to see him against a background.

"I think you mentioned that one of your great-great-grandfathers was a sea captain," she ventured.

"That's the one. Jackson Matthew Powers, the original. Back in the days of sail, he ran the West Indies route, hauling mostly rice, rum, sugar, molasses and lumber. There were a few yellowed old manifestos tucked between the pages of the ledger. The old guy wasn't much of a bookkeeper."

"You said something about a coincidence?"

"About the babies. You know, it's the damnedest thing. I never thought much about it before—I mean, it was an interesting story, but I was more interested at fifteen in tales of storms weathered and waterfront brawls, and how the old man assured himself of a crew when he left port by jailing them all after the first night of hell raising, whether they deserved it or not."

"Mercy, he doesn't sound like a pleasant character."

"Those were tough days. He might even have saved a few lives by preventing trouble before it broke out."

"Where does the baby come in?"

"Okay, I'm not too clear on this, but as I understand it, for some unspecified reason he put his ship up for sale and settled on the Outer Banks at a place called Powers Point when he was still a relatively young man. Some of his crew settled there with him, in what started out to be an all-male household.''

''There must have been at least one woman somewhere,'' Hetty observed.

Motorized carts were beeping past as passengers were transported to their respective gates. Jax glanced up at the monitor, then flexed his hands. Hetty stared at them, trying to forget how warm and strong they'd felt on her body.

''Where was I? Oh, yeah…women. There were several, matter of fact, but the one that started the trouble was married to a fisherman from the nearest village. It seems the lady took a shine to my great-great-grandfather's first mate. One day about a year after they'd settled ashore, the lady's husband came to Powers Point. He was carrying a brand-new baby under one arm and a shotgun under the other. Seemed his wife had confessed to having an affair with the young seaman. Evidently, the fisherman wasn't, uh—sufficiently productive—and he suspected the kid wasn't his.''

Sunny started to whimper in her sleep, and both Jax and Hetty reached out at the same time to comfort her. Their hands met on the baby's stomach. She would've pulled hers back, but he captured her fingers and refused to release them.

''Shh, don't wake her up,'' he murmured.

He held on to her hand, and both of them watched the board because neither dared look at the other. There it was again, that shivery sense of being connected by a powerful, invisible bond.

"What happened?" she whispered.

"Happened? Oh, yeah, the baby. Well, as near as I can make out, something pretty bad happened that day that ended up with the old guy—my great-great-grandfather—of course he was younger then, becoming the official guardian of a newborn baby girl. Can you beat it?"

"What happened next?"

He shrugged. And then he dropped her hand and sat up straight. "Hey, what do you know, I think we just got lucky. Hang tight and let me see what I can work out, will you?"

Strange, how lonely one could feel in the midst of thousands of people. Hetty watched until Jax disappeared into the crowd, then edged closer to Sunny's carrier. She made up her mind to see them off with a smile if it killed her. Once they were gone she would put into effect her own plan, which so far consisted solely of demanding, insisting, whining and complaining. It had always worked for Jeannie.

Except for a few sleepy sounds and some smacking of the gums, Sunny slept through it all. After a while Hetty lifted her from the carrier and cradled the warm body in her arms for no other reason than that she needed the comfort of holding someone close.

She watched for Jax to reappear. Searched for a glimpse of his dark head, that proud, beard-shadowed face with the square jaw, the arched nose and the deep-set, dark-blue eyes.

And then she saw him. He was standing at the service desk, speaking rapidly with a uniformed attendant. He smiled and nodded, and her heart sank.

Forcing herself to concentrate on her own plan, she wondered which to try first. The woman at the console or the traveler's aid lady. Traveler's aid might be the best bet. They were probably used to dealing with stranded travelers, else the airports would all be filled with homeless wanderers.

Jax had mentioned a proposition. That could mean most anything, but in a man-woman context, it usually had only one meaning. She hadn't dared ask.

But the answer was "no." No way, under no circumstances. Not because she didn't want to, but because she had better sense.

Once before she had let herself be rescued from an impossible situation by a man. Gus had come along just as she was thinking of running away from home to escape her father. She had known Gus all her life, but only the way people in small towns knew other people by sight or reputation. He'd been a Vietnam veteran. A pilot, a hero, some said.

He had certainly turned out to be a hero where she was concerned. She'd been seeing him for years in Olesen's Hardware. She remembered thinking he was nice looking, for an older man. Then one day he drove out to deliver a barrel of heating oil, and he'd seen her with badly bruised arms, a black eye and a swollen lip. And he'd known, because Vern Reynolds's temper and his drinking were no secret around town.

So he'd taken her home to his mother, and a few days later they'd been married. She had spent the next eleven years as his wife, being treated with kindness and an affection that had helped her to heal. She had looked after his mother, who was frail and a little silly, but wonderfully kind. She had done her best with his young daughter, trying hard to overcome the child's natural resentment. She had been as good a wife to Gus as any frightened, inexperienced young girl could be to a man more than twice her age.

It had been a busy but safe and comfortable life. With her mother-in-law's advice, she had learned to be a better cook, to sew, to deal with a rebellious teenager. She had watched her husband eat his supper in silence every night and then doze in front of TV in his work clothes and sock feet. On Friday nights they would go upstairs and make love quietly so as not to disturb either Sadie or Jeannie.

It had been pleasant. Gus had always fallen asleep immediately afterward, but he'd never failed to thank her the next morning, which she thought was incredibly sweet.

When he'd been killed, she'd held the family together. When Jeannie had started getting in trouble at school and staying out all night, she had dealt with it the best way she knew how.

When Sadie had suffered the first of a series of strokes, she had dealt with that, as well, and when Jeannie had run away, she'd been torn between chasing after her and nursing Sadie.

And then Jeannie had brought her Robert, and between Sadie and the baby, she had *really* had her hands full.

She would go back, because it was the proper thing to do. And because she had nowhere else to go. And because family was important, and she missed Robert.

But this time she would remain independent. Never again would she risk depending on anyone other than herself.

Five

"It's all settled. You've got a seat on the flight that leaves at 3:10 for Norfolk." Jax looked as smug as if he'd just pulled off a major coup.

As indeed he probably had. It hadn't taken long for Hetty to discover she could be here for hours, if not days. Half the people around her were clamoring to change their itinerary, their original plans having been ruined by the delay. They'd been arguing the point ever since he'd come back to tell her what he'd done on her behalf.

"I haven't actually said I'd do it, not in so many words."

"Anyone ever call you stubborn?"

"Stubborn can be a good trait."

"Not if it's taken to unreasonable lengths. Hetty, you know it's the right thing to do. Sunny needs you. She's used to you. What the devil am I supposed to do for the next few days until I can make other arrangements? Take her to the office with me? Sneak her into an adults-only apartment complex? Bring in a baby-sitter I don't know from Adam and entrust her with my child?"

She couldn't answer his question, and so she asked one of her own. "Why would anyone want to live in a place that doesn't allow children?"

He closed his eyes momentarily. Hetty knew his head still ached, by now she recognized the signs. She also knew she gave new definition to the word *pig-headed,* because she'd been told as much on more than a few occasions by both her father and her step-daughter.

But it was important to learn all she could before she agreed to anything, because the last time she'd acted on impulse it had turned into a major fiasco. Which was why she was here in the first place.

"Well?" she persisted. "I know all about condos and apartments full of swinging singles—my mother-in-law used to watch daytime TV. I don't really think you're that kind of man, but all the same, if I'm going to do this thing I need to know everything there is to know about what I'm letting myself in for."

He shook his head slowly. The look on his face said, I can't believe I'm having this conversation.

But then, neither could she.

"Because I needed a place to live," he said tiredly.

"Because it's conveniently located. Hell, how do I know? I've never had to explain my choices before. Now, are you going to help us out, or are you going to take up permanent residence in Chicago?"

"It probably wouldn't have cost any more to get me a ticket back to Oklahoma City. I'd have paid you back."

"Not a chance, honey. You wouldn't have made it out anytime soon, and I don't want you hanging around this place any longer. The clincher is that I already had two tickets to Norfolk. I bought Sunny and her carrier a separate seat, but legally she's still young enough to fly on my ticket."

"Then why did you buy two?"

"Because it's a damned long way from California to Virginia," he snapped. "Hetty, are you doing this deliberately?"

"No, I only want to be sure I know all the details before I commit to anything."

Her father would have whopped her across the face long before now. Jeannie would've locked herself in her room with a pack of cigarettes, a jar of peanut butter and a telephone. *Patience* wasn't a word that could be used to describe either of them.

Jax took a deep breath and went over it all again. "I'm going to have to find a baby-sitter, a house and a housekeeper, in that order. Meanwhile, I'll be transferring as much of my caseload as possible to Jason." He'd mentioned the junior partner of his small maritime law firm before. "I'm not sure I can do all that needs doing while I'm holding a baby in one arm."

"Well...I don't know," she stalled.

He took one of his daughter's tiny feet in his hand. "See, Sunshine? What'd I tell you? Stubborn as a mule. You sure this is the one you want?"

Hetty didn't want to smile, because she was still terribly uncertain if this was the right thing to do. If he had an ulterior motive, she couldn't imagine what it could be.

And if he didn't...well, she might be disappointed, but it wouldn't be the first time.

As if taking her acquiescence for granted, Jax began gathering up Sunny's paraphernalia, his coat and briefcase. "Face it, Henrietta, we both got lucky. If the weather hadn't fouled up, I'd be in Norfolk now, trying to figure out how to juggle work and single parenthood. You'd be cruising the Caribbean in all your fine feathers, breaking hearts and fielding proposals."

She muttered "horse manure," which was tantamount to surrender.

Jax knew it, too, judging by his tired grin. Hetty said, "Well, all right, but it's strictly temporary. And I'm only doing it for Sunny's sake, because she deserves someone who knows something about babies."

"Great! What do you have to lose?"

What did she have to lose? Only everything. She might act foolishly on rare occasions, but she was no fool. She was wildly attracted to a man who would use her until he no longer needed her, then walk away without a backward glance. Because in spite of her fancy clothes and new hairstyle, Hetty knew she wasn't the kind of woman men looked back at.

The fact that she'd literally slept with him a few times didn't help matters. He'd been aroused, but that was a normal, male-morning thing. She'd been aroused because…well, just because. Naturally they hadn't made love, but she couldn't help wondering what might have happened if the circumstances had been different.

Neither could she help wondering about Sunny's mother. Had they been married? Was he divorced? Separated? Had she died? Was he still in love with her?

"Well," she said decisively, having made up her mind to look on the practical side. It was a job, and she needed employment, even temporary employment, if she was ever going to get back to Oklahoma. "I guess it won't hurt to delay my own plans for a few more days."

They boarded some forty-five minutes later. The plane was filled to capacity, carry-on baggage limited to Jax's briefcase and Sunny's bulky diaper bag. They'd checked the carrier at the gate. The flight attendant promised milk and snacks the minute they reached cruising altitude and slipped Jax a package of pretzels for Sunny to chew on.

Lost in their own separate thoughts, neither spoke as the plane picked up speed down the runway. They lifted off, and Hetty closed her eyes, clinging to the armrests in a white-knuckled grip. Not until they were in the air did she release the breath she'd been holding.

Moments later she felt two distinct thuds somewhere in the belly of the monstrous plane and fought panic all over again.

Jax covered her hand with one of his own. "Relax, it's only the wheel flaps."

"I knew that," she said, trying hard to turn abject fear into a joking matter.

"Sure you did. It's when it doesn't happen that you start to worry."

"Yes, well...I didn't notice it when we left Oklahoma City, but that was back in the old days, when flying was still an adventure."

He chuckled and settled Sunny more comfortably on his lap. He'd taken the window seat at Hetty's insistence when she'd told him she'd rather not see how far off the ground she was. "As soon as the seatbelt light goes off, you might want to check out the john. I've heard there's real soap there."

"No shower?"

"Don't be greedy."

"Okay, I'll go first and wash up, but if they start serving before I get back, grab me two of everything."

"You got it." His smile was tired, but warm. "Don't know much about airline food, do you?"

"Enough to know it's better than no food at all."

She would like to believe there was more than amusement in his smile, but then, she'd read somewhere that extreme hunger could make a person delusional.

The flight was surprisingly uneventful. "Those people across the aisle are sleeping," Hetty murmured. "I don't think I could ever be that blasé about sleeping in public."

"I dunno, you did pretty well on the floor back at O'Hare.

"Only because I was exhausted and there was nowhere else."

"Actually, there was a hotel, but by the time I could get a bid in, it was filled to capacity. We were probably better off where we were."

"I couldn't have done it alone. I mean, sleeping and all." Her color had improved while she was devouring chicken à la airline. Now it flared up again. "You know what I mean," she mumbled, embarrassed, and Jax assured her that he did.

He was still trying to convince himself that he wasn't making a mistake. He'd used Sunny as an excuse, but his secretary could've arranged some interim solution. There were bonded temps for almost everything these days.

The practical side of his brain said it was a logical solution to both their problems.

Another side—the same one that had prompted him to buy the *Lizzie-Linda,* was whipping out warnings he was trying hard to ignore.

The plain truth was, he wanted her. Not the glamorous creature he'd mistaken her for at first, but the unpretentious woman he'd discovered as he got to know her better.

Or maybe it was the combination that intrigued him. He had never before met a woman who was both naive and experienced. Who looked like a high-fashion model, but whose hands had obviously done their share of manual labor.

Hell, she'd even done Sunny's laundry in the rest room. Washed her blankets and a couple of sleepers, scrubbing her knuckles raw to make up for the lack of soap.

He could almost see her as one of those pioneer women who plowed and planted alongside their husbands, who bore children and raised them and grew old well before their time. She might look frail, but hers was the strength of endurance.

God, he hoped he wasn't making a mistake. He didn't know where this thing was leading. He knew where he wanted it to lead, but the more he was tempted, the warier be became. Walking away from an affair with Hetty, if that's where this ended up, would not be a simple matter.

Sunny was sleeping when they touched down and taxied up to the gate, her little belly filled with warm milk, scrambled eggs and biscotti. She continued to sleep while they waited until after the worst of the crush was past, then followed the last few straggling passengers. She was turning out to be a surprisingly hardy little sprout.

Jax left them at one of the ground transportation

exits while he went to collect his car. Now that her ordeal was nearing an end, Hetty was almost too exhausted to move, but Jax was counting on her to take care of Sunny, so she braced her shoulders and tried not to think about a long, hot soak and a soft, clean bed.

The Sunny-filled carrier was heavy, but Hetty didn't dare set it down, not with so many people hurrying past. Poor mite was beginning to fuss again. Wet, probably. There'd been no room to change her on the plane, and no clean diapers. She suspected Jax was used to flying first class, where there was more room, but on this particular airline there was no first class.

"Here he comes, sweety pie," she said, spotting the familiar dark head dodging buses, taxis and shuttles. "It won't be long now."

Jax took the carrier from her, tickled his daughter under the chin and said, "It won't be long now, we're in the home stretch." He took Hetty's arm, cautioned her to watch the curb, then his hand slid down, and he laced his fingers through hers, leading her to an elegant dark sedan.

Catching sight of an attractive woman staring at him with hungry, speculative eyes, Hetty felt a surge of possessive pride.

Talk about courting disaster.

The first few evening stars were visible when he pulled up in front of the hotel and handed his keys over to the valet. Calling ahead from his car, he had booked a suite of rooms: two bedrooms, two baths, with a living room between. "I ordered a crib set up in your room, is that okay?"

"Certainly. That's what I'm here for," Hetty said quietly.

Jax was no longer quite so certain why she was here, but this was no time to delve into ulterior motives. Hers or his own.

The bellman let them into the suite, set down their luggage, which consisted only of a briefcase and diaper bag, then adjusted the heat, palmed a tip and left.

Jax loosened his necktie, which by now was beyond redemption. "I'll keep watch here while you freshen up. Why not look over the menu first and tell me what you want. I'll order us some supper."

Hetty had already checked out the bathroom. "It's going to take a long, hot soak to freshen me up. Half an hour, at least, but first I'd better see what I can do about Sunny. What do you think, a hand towel? It'll be bulky, but at least it's dry." She lifted the drowsy baby from the carrier. "Come on, sugar-bun, let's make you all comfy and then Poppa will go find you some milk, cereal and lots of nice, dry diapers."

Jax opened the small refrigerator. He produced a bottle of orange juice and set it on the bar. "Poppa?" he repeated softly.

"She can't quite manage *father* yet. Oh, good, she'll love orange juice. Robert did."

Jax had heard about all he cared to hear about her stepgrandson. To hear her tell it, Robert was practically scholarship material before he was three months old.

But he didn't say so, because he wasn't churlish by nature, and because he didn't like what it implied about his present state of mind.

Once she'd finished settling Sunny, he handed her a menu and watched while she read over the offerings, scanned them again, then mentioned the cheapest thing listed.

He called in the order, adding two appetizers, two desserts, a pot of coffee and a bottle of wine.

"Is half an hour too long?" she asked anxiously. "I could just shower."

"Take all the time you need, this time of night, room service will be pretty slow."

"I'll make it quick, just in case."

He'd ordered wine. Hetty didn't drink beer, wine or anything stronger, not with her early introduction to alcoholism, but she didn't make an issue of it. At the moment she lacked the energy to make an issue of anything.

Not until she lowered herself into the steaming tub of water did it strike her that sleeping with a stranger on the floor of a public building was one thing, but sharing a meal and a hotel suite with the same man was something altogether different. Especially now that she'd got to know the man behind those Hollywood handsome looks. She liked him. Not only was she wildly attracted to him, she genuinely liked him.

She'd liked Gus, too, of course, and learned to love him for the sweet, decent man he was. And while Jax was sweet and decent, what she was beginning to feel for him bore no resemblance to the mild, pleasant relationship she'd had with her husband.

Hetty told herself she'd do well to mind her p's and q's. And then she spent the next five minutes soaking in heavenly bliss, trying drowsily to remember what p's and q's were. She vaguely remembered reading about it somewhere in the distant past. Something to do with typesetting....

"Hetty? You all right in there?"

"Wha—?"

"If you're going to fall asleep in a tubful of water, I'd better see if I can find you a pair of water wings. Supper's here, in case you're interested."

Jax heard splashing and muttering, then heard water gurgling down the drain. "There should be a bathrobe behind the door," he called through the door.

"I didn't even think—yes, there is. Thanks, I'll be out in two minutes."

She was as good as her word. Jax knew damned well he had dined under more difficult circumstances, but at the moment he couldn't recall when or where. Sitting across the small table from a woman who was wearing only a thick white terry cloth robe, her wet hair wrapped in a towel, her bare feet propped on a third chair, was enough to get a rise from a dead man. And Jax wasn't quite dead yet.

Worried, yes. Bone tired, too, which was only to be expected. But damned if she didn't turn him on doing no more than gnawing a chicken bone and licking her fingers.

"Did you find diapers and formula?" Earlier, leaving Sunny asleep in her crib, he'd called through her door that he was going to check out the drugstore just off the lobby.

"Laid in a supply."

"She's been amazingly patient. Pass me the ketchup, will you?" A grand cru chablis and ketchup on her fries. The lady was an enigma. "Robert was always colicky," she remarked.

"Is that a fact?" He tried to look sympathetic, but he couldn't help feeling smug. He was going to have to watch this baby-pride stuff, or he'd turn into one of those parents who hauled out snapshots at the drop of a hat.

"Babies react to tension just like anyone else. My mother-in-law was sick the whole time I had Robert—well, actually more incapacitated than sick, but she demanded a lot of attention. And I was worried about Jeannie, so it was probably no wonder Robert cried a lot. Poor little thing, he was such a fussy eater."

He couldn't help himself. He grinned. New fathers were allowed a little latitude, weren't they? "Sunny's pretty unflappable. That's a sign of a well-adjusted personality, wouldn't you say?"

She glanced up at him through a sweep of long, golden-tipped lashes. The look was innocent, mildly speculative, not at all flirtatious. "Not necessarily. Jax, if I'm supposed to be looking after her these next few days, is there anything I should know? About her background, I mean?"

A few days? Jax didn't remember setting any limits. He considered satisfying her curiosity, told himself it was none of her business, then said, "Carolyn's perfectly normal, healthy, no allergies or health problems, mental or physical, that I know of. And in answer to the questions you're too polite to ask, she and I had a brief affair about eighteen months ago. I didn't know her well at the time and haven't spoken to her since, until she called to tell me we had a daughter."

Looking thoughtful, Hetty reached for one of the triple-chocolate sundaes topped with raspberry sauce. "So why did she give away her baby?"

"She didn't 'give her away,' as you put it. She's leaving the country for an extended stay and decided Sunny would be better off in a more stable situation." He didn't mention the fact that if he hadn't taken her, Carolyn had planned to put her up for adoption.

"That's so sad. For Carolyn, I mean. I can't imagine anything more painful than having to give up a child. I only had Robert five months, but leaving him was the most painful thing I've ever had to do. Did you tell her that people travel all the time with babies? They're remarkably adaptable."

"I didn't tell her anything. I don't know whether they're adaptable or not. I took Sunny because I want her, and now, if the interrogation is finished, shall we polish off the wine?" He'd had three glasses. She had barely tasted hers.

Sunny's adaptability evidently had its limits. Jax woke in the middle of the night to hear Hetty softly

crooning the song about looking glasses and mockingbirds. Pulling on his slacks, he moved silently to
the door and opened it, wishing he'd taken the time
to go across town to his own place to pack a bag. He
hadn't, only because it would have been unfair to
Hetty, as she hadn't had time yet to shop.

He made a mental note to call Lina, his secretary,
first thing in the morning and have her take Hetty
shopping. The thought of outfitting her from the skin
out triggered images he could do without. Even so,
for a long time he stood and watched from the shadows of the doorway.

She was still wearing the bulky terry cloth robe.
She couldn't have slept in the thing, it would hog-tie
her the first time she rolled over.

Unbidden, his imagination took over once more,
screening pictures of a nude Hetty sliding between
silken sheets. He happened to know she slept on her
side. She didn't snore, but when she was deeply
asleep she made soft, puffy little noises with her lips.

He swore softly and backed away. If just seeing
her like this got to him until he was so hard he hurt,
he'd damned well better start looking for a house and
a staff before he did anything else.

If he was going to get involved—big *if*—he would
have to be sure it was for his own sake, not his daughter's. Not that he was even considering marriage, but
if he did—another big *if*—it damn well wouldn't be
any marriage of convenience.

"'Hush, little baby, don't you cry, Mama's gonna
rock you bye and bye.'"

Rocking chair. Yeah, he'd see about getting one of those, too, he told himself as the whispery sound of Hetty's voice followed him into the bedroom.

Hours later, his head aching, his eyes burning, Jax stared up at the ceiling and tried to pinpoint the precise time his well-ordered life had begun to spin out of control.

Six

Hetty would've given anything for concealer, blusher and lipstick. Jax had brought her a toothbrush, toothpaste, comb and a hairbrush from the drugstore last night and asked if she needed anything else before morning.

She could have mentioned several items. Deodorant. Nightgown. Clean underwear. Her old life back.

Instead, she'd sponged her skirt and mended the rip, using the hotel's sewing kit. She'd rinsed out her underwear before she went to bed, then had lain awake, listening to Sunny's breathing. Listening to Jax in the next room talking to someone on the phone. Trying to convince herself she wasn't making a monumental mistake.

She had a family back in Oklahoma. She could never be one of those independent women who didn't need her family. And whether or not her family realized it, they needed her, too.

Back and forth, back and forth, go or stay...

When morning finally came, nothing had changed. She was still feeling wary, vulnerable—afraid to go forward, afraid to go back. Most of all, afraid she was falling deeper in love with every passing day.

Her underwear was still damp, but she put it on, anyway. Whether she liked it or not—and she didn't—she was going to need another loan. She could call it an advance on her salary, only they'd never got around to discussing the terms, much less the duration, of her employment.

Among several recent changes in her life, one stood out in stark relief—gone was the thirst for travel and adventure that had first driven her to jump at the chance to fly to Miami and board a cruise ship. Totally evaporated.

Unfortunately the dream that had crept in like a thief in the night to take its place involved a husband and a baby. Maybe two babies. His and hers. Theirs.

Which was hardly a realistic dream for a woman of Hetty's age, but then, that was the nice thing about dreams. They didn't have to be realistic. Before she'd even learned how to dream, she'd had her once-in-a-lifetime fairy-tale romance. Gus had come along like a knight in shining armor at a time when she'd been in desperate need of rescuing. She'd been too embarrassed to ask for help, but somehow Gus had known.

Over coffee, she said, "Jax, as far as I know, my luggage is somewhere between Oklahoma and Florida. I'm going to need—"

"All taken care of." With the smug expression of a cat in a creamery he told her he'd put a tracer on her baggage and that meanwhile, his secretary would be there within the hour, bringing a selection of clothes for Hetty to choose from so that she would have something to wear while she shopped for whatever else she needed.

Hetty slammed her cup down. "Darn it, don't *do* this to me!"

"What, you want to go shopping in sandals and that floppy thing you're wearing now? It's about thirty-four degrees Fahrenheit outside and windy."

He had a point. Her clothes, while they might be fine for a Caribbean cruise, were hardly suited for a January rain. She spun around and glared out at the gray drizzle coming down outside. "This is just not working."

"It's working fine. Climb down off your high horse and listen for a minute, will you? Lina will—"

"You paid for my ticket. You—"

"You looked after my daughter."

"You bought me food, you bought me—"

"That's where you're mistaken. I offered to trade what you need for what I need. It's called the barter system. It's a recognized and respectable custom all over the world."

"Yes, well...but—"

"I'm listening." He crossed his arms over his

chest. His jaw had that clean-shaven, early-morning look, even though he was still wearing the same rumpled shirt and baggy-kneed flannels he'd worn since day one.

It made her feel marginally better that he hadn't raced home last night to shower and change. Misery liked company. "I hate being in debt. My—that is, someone ran up a huge bill on my credit card once, and I had to pay for it."

"If you'd reported it immediately, you'd have been responsible for only about fifty bucks."

"Yes, but Jeannie might have—"

She clammed up, but not before he got the picture. Evidently that stepdaughter of hers was a real piece of work. "Believe me, Hetty, you'll earn every penny I pay you. Now, here's what I've got planned for today. First, I'll need to run by my apartment to collect clothes and mail."

He'd already collected his messages. He'd still been on the phone when she'd fallen asleep last night.

"Give me—say, two hours. Meanwhile, Lina will bring over a raincoat and a pair of sensible shoes—size eight, narrow, right?"

"You looked!"

"So sue me." His grin was wickedly attractive. "I'll be back in time to watch Sunny while you two go shopping. After that I have in mind leaving you here while I start negotiating for a house. Once that's in the works, I'll get started on hiring staff."

He peered at her closed face, looking for some clue that she was going to be reasonable. "The thing is, all this takes time, and I'm in the middle of a big case right now, with several smaller ones coming to a head. In other words, I'm going to be tied up for the next few weeks, and I need someone I can trust to look after my daughter.''

She flung out her hands. "Jackson, that's just it! I'm a stranger, someone you picked up in an airport. How can you trust me not to—to—''

"You can't even think of an appropriate crime, can you? How about kidnapping Sunny and holding her for ransom?''

"Be serious.''

"I am serious. I trust you. Maybe not right at first, because you looked like a—''

"Like a fool, dressed for a Caribbean cruise in the middle of a blizzard.''

"Because you looked like a fashion model. Beautiful, but without the vacant stare.'' He narrowed his eyes. "What? Why are you looking at me like that?''

"You thought I was beautiful? But I'm not. I never have been.''

"I didn't say you were pretty. There's a difference between being pretty and being beautiful, and don't ask me what it is because I can't explain it. The important thing is, I got to know you and I learned to trust you, and dammit, Hetty, I need you!''

They'd left it at that. The day had gone precisely as he'd arranged it. And as tired as she was, it felt good to know she could change from the skin out into clean clothes and still have a spare in case Sunny spit up on her.

"That's right, sugar-britches, Daa-daa. Maa-maa."

Sunny stared up at her, her huge, dark blue eyes unfocused as she tried to interpret whatever message this odd creature was attempting to impart.

"Never mind, Daddy can learn to answer to "Goo-umble-umm.""

They had practiced sitting up. Sunny was wobbly, but she was ready. She'd already mastered the art of scooting across the floor on one knee, both hands and her bottom. There'd be no holding her back after this.

Later, while Sunny napped, Hetty took the opportunity to soak in a tubful of hot water, reading a chapter of the paperback novel Lina had recommended. It was a luxury she'd seldom had the opportunity to indulge in back in Minco, thanks to a lack of time and an elderly, inefficient hot water heater.

Sighing, she laid the book aside and closed her eyes. Every bone and muscle in her body ached, whether from all the shopping she'd done today or sleeping on a strange bed last night or from simply an accumulation of those plus sleeping on a hard airport floor in Chicago.

Old bones. She'd heard the phrase more than once. Now she knew firsthand what it meant.

Lina had been surprised—disappointed, Hetty suspected—when she'd insisted on going to a discount department store and buying the basics—two pairs of jeans, one dark knit skirt, three tops, an all-weather coat that made up in practicality what it lacked in beauty. She'd splurged on a three-day supply of plain cotton underwear and the necessary toiletries, and then headed for the infant department.

"Hold on, you're going to need at least two night-gowns, and what about a bathrobe?" the older woman had reminded her.

"I'll sleep in a T-shirt. As for a bathrobe, the hotel provides a lovely one."

"Huh! Well, at least get yourself two pairs of good shoes and some slippers."

"One pair of shoes, no slippers."

"You don't know who's walked on those hotel carpets before. They don't shampoo them between guests, you know."

"So I'll wear socks if I get up in the night."

"You'll get up all right, unless babies have changed since mine were that age. I don't understand you, Henrietta, I just don't. Jax is paying. He's going to blame me for bringing you here."

"How long have you worked for him?"

"Ever since he first set up office. He's two years younger than my oldest boy, but we took to each other right off."

Hetty would have placed the secretary's age in the midfifties. She revised it a few years upward. A large woman with a nice sense of style, Lina's gray hair was cut in a sassy young wedge that was both daring and flattering. Hetty had been so proud of her own new haircut. Compared to Lina's, it was small-town dowdy.

But then, so was she.

"I only met him a few days ago," she confessed. "I guess he told you about how we met and how I came to be here." She refused to sail under false colors. Lina had been hinting all morning at a relationship that simply didn't exist. Nor was it ever likely to. "I'm only temporary, until he can find someone better. We have this barter thing going, so you see, I won't be here long enough to earn more than the basics. Besides, Jax said he'd put a tracer on my baggage. Once that comes..."

Once that came, if it ever did, she'd have several pairs of summer pants, several tropical-print tops, one long skirt, plus shorts, camp shirts, bathing suits and the usual accessories.

At the infant-and-children's section, Hetty insisted on buying several outfits for Sunny. When she'd discovered how little the child had, she'd asked Jax about it. He'd shrugged and said, "Carolyn said she outgrew things so fast there was no point in sending her old things, that I'd probably need to buy everything new in a larger size."

Hetty knew for a fact that babies could outgrow things almost overnight. All the same, she was beginning to believe Sunny had been sorely neglected, in more ways than one. She was almost too undemanding.

She added a snowsuit in a larger size to the growing pile. "He won't mind, will he?" she asked Lina as the two women stacked their purchases on the checkout counter.

"Lord, no. He's generous to a fault, but he's got a

lot to learn when it comes to taking care of a baby.'' She took out a platinum card and watched like a hawk as the purchases were rung up. "Women, too. I probably shouldn't be telling you this, and if it was about his work, you couldn't pry my jaws apart, but you might as well know that when it comes to women, that boy doesn't have a speck of judgment. He won't talk about his family—I'm not sure he even has one, but if he had no more brains than to get involved with the kind of woman who would give her baby away just so she could go traipsing off around the world, then the good Lord help him. If you ask me, she probably spent every cent she had on her own back. Babies aren't cheap, you know. In my day we washed diapers and used them until they wore out, then used them as dust rags. All my babies ate regular food, strained and mashed in my own kitchen, not all this special stuff.''

At least there was nothing wrong with Sunny's appetite. Hetty had stocked up on Robert's favorite foods, and Sunny had yet to refuse anything. "Tomorrow we'll go shopping for a stroller and a playpen, sugar-bun,'' Hetty promised now, burying her face in Sunny's warm, plump belly just to hear her gurgling laughter.

She was still smiling when she heard Jax let himself into the suite. He'd left as soon as she and Lina had returned from their shopping spree. Since then she hadn't heard a word from him. In spite of all her common-sense resolutions, there was nothing she could do about the sudden leap of her heart.

* * *

Jax let himself inside the room quietly in case Sunny was sleeping. Since he'd left that morning, he had packed enough clothes for several days, dealt with the mail and the latest batch of phone messages at his apartment. They'd all been of a personal nature, including one from the woman he was currently seeing, reminding him of the birthday dinner he'd promised her.

He'd clean forgotten it.

Next, he'd met with a real estate agent to spell out his requirements, talked at length to a representative of the shipping firm that owned the vessel involved in the October oil spill, to the Coast Guard exec in charge of the cleanup and to someone from the governmental Oil Spill Liability Trust Fund.

He'd dealt with two minor cases, taped responses to several letters for Lina to transcribe and gone shopping for a birthday gift suitable for a woman with whom he'd shared a lackadaisical six-month affair.

While he was at the jeweler's, he'd impulsively selected a sterling silver mug and had it engraved, "To Sunny from Daddy, with love."

"Hi, is she asleep?" he whispered, closing the door silently behind him.

"I just put her down again. She's still making noises. I think she's practicing to surprise you with her vocabulary."

"What vocabulary? I haven't heard anything that sounded like words yet."

"That's because you don't know what to listen for."

Jax tried not to stare at the tall, elegant creature with the cheekbones and the big, rain-colored eyes. She was wearing the same old terry cloth robe. On her it looked sexy as the devil.

Which just went to show that he'd pushed the limits today, after a night in which he hadn't slept more than a few hours.

He dropped his briefcase on the French Provincial desk and crossed to the miniature bar. "Drink?"

"I made coffee."

"I need something stronger. Have you eaten yet?"

"No, I—"

"I'll order. I skipped lunch. What do you feel like tonight, steak? Seafood?"

What she felt like was something homey, like stewed chicken and biscuits, something that didn't make her feel so much like an imposter. Which was ironic for someone who, if things had worked out, would have been dining on the high seas tonight on such exotic fare as lobster and caviar.

She said, "Maybe chicken again."

It was the strangest thing. Hetty couldn't quite put her finger on it, but something was different. Tonight they sat across the table, dining together on a room-service dinner, neither of them listening to the all-news station Jax had turned on when he'd first come in.

They'd done more or less the same thing last night, but then they'd both been exhausted, travel-stained and worried.

Tonight was different. It could have been the hot

bath, or the sip or two of wine—she hated to waste anything that cost so much. Whatever the cause, for reasons she couldn't begin to understand, Hetty was acutely aware of her body in a way she hadn't been since the early days of her marriage.

"Did you find everything you needed today?" He broke off half a roll and topped it with butter.

"Mercy, more than enough. Wait'll you see the bills."

"Have some more wine."

"No, thank you. I thought about getting a stroller and a playpen, but decided I'd better ask you first."

Jax topped off her wineglass, which had hardly been touched, then watched as she sipped it. She tilted her head as if surprised, then sipped again. "You know, it's not at all bad once you get used to it. The only other wine I've ever tasted was sickly sweet."

"Buy whatever you need. Lina can tell you where I have accounts."

"I spent an enormous amount today, I hope you don't mind. And you need to know in case you ever have to buy diapers again that they come in two different styles. Girls and boys."

"You're kidding." He said it flatly, replacing the wine bottle in the cooler. "Pink and blue, you mean?"

"Well, there's that, but it's—they're padded in different places. You see—well, I don't know how much you know about anatomy," she said, and then slapped a hand over her face.

"About as much as the average forty-year-old, I guess," he said blandly.

"What I meant was—oh, for heaven's sake, just buy the pink ones!"

Then he was laughing, and Hetty was, too, and she blamed it on the wine and on the hot bath and on the romance she'd been reading. Blamed it on everything except the truth.

That she was wildly attracted to the man, and seeing him again and again under the most intimate circumstances made it almost impossible to keep her imagination in check.

"Okay, pink diapers, stroller, playpen—whatever she needs. Did you get yourself some pretty things? A warm coat and a pair of boots, I hope."

"I got everything I need, and thank you very much. Did you have any luck finding a house? Because you must know this place is costing you an arm and a leg, and if you've already got an apartment in town, then you could move us into something smaller and cheaper and then you can—"

"Hetty."

She broke off. "What?"

"You're chattering."

He was staring at her. He'd been staring at her for several minutes. It was making her nervous, because she was trying so hard not to stare at him.

The man was devastating. So what if his features were just short of perfection, the sum total was every bit as intoxicating as the wine she was drinking on practically an empty stomach.

"You didn't eat your chicken."

"I wasn't as hungry as I thought."

"Is that what's making you so edgy?"

She was tempted to tell him the truth. Scrambling for a reasonable excuse, she said, "New shoes."

"Oh. You're talking too much because you bought some new shoes, is that it?"

"I'm talking too much because I have a blister on my left heel and because you make me nervous, and because—"

"Hetty," he said in a voice as soft as midnight fog.

"What?" she practically snarled.

"Give me your foot."

"I'm not giving you anything! I've already given you far too much." His eyebrows rose at that, and she hastened to explain, only making matters worse. "I mean, you know my whole life history, and I don't know anything at all about you except that your great-great-grandfather was a sea captain who gave up the sea and adopted a baby girl."

"Give me your foot."

"Jax, you might as well know I'm not really as glamorous as I look, it's the clothes." She plucked at the bulky bathrobe. "Not this, but my other things. You know what I mean. I bought all these glamorous new things for my cruise because I didn't have anything the least bit suitable, and—well—underneath, I'm really just plain old Hetty Reynolds, who's never been anywhere or done anything the least bit exciting."

He'd pretty well figured that out all by himself. He

resisted the urge to haul her into his arms and hold her until both of them came to their senses, because, glamorous or not, there was something about the woman that brought out a protective streak he hadn't known he possessed.

"I know," he said gently, warming her with his eyes.

"And I'm not used to staying in hotels. If you want to know the truth, I've never stayed in one before in my life. Motels, yes, but they don't have room service, much less all these little goodies. All this is—" She waved her arms, and Jax reached under the table, captured one of her feet and lifted it onto his knee.

"D'you know what killed Calvin Coolidge?"

She goggled at him. There was no other way to describe it.

"Blister on his foot. Infection set in, and next thing you know, he was gone."

"You're making that up."

"Now why would I do a thing like that?"

With his hard, dry palms stroking her foot, she could hardly remember the question, much less think of an answer.

"To educate you?" His fingers massaged her ticklish arch.

"Ah, mmm…"

"To entertain you?"

"Oh, well…"

"Hetty, if I wanted to entertain you, I could think of a number of better ways. Hmm. Skin's not broken.

Your heel's pink, though. We'll have to get you a bandage.''

He folded the flap of her robe back over her knee, replaced her foot on the floor and reached for her hand. As if mesmerized, she let him pull her to her feet and draw her into his arms.

It had to be the wine, she thought distractedly.

Not true. It's the man.

The kiss began gently, almost as if he was afraid of frightening her. By the time Jax took her chin between thumb and forefinger and tilted her face for a better advantage, Hetty had surrendered to the inevitable. They had been heading toward this moment for days, ever since he had kissed her at the airport.

Thinking about it.

Trying so hard *not* to think about it.

He tasted of wine and chocolate and something far more delicious, far more intoxicating. It never occurred to her to hold back. Whatever mysterious forces had led her here, to this man, this moment, they were beyond her power to resist. Far from resisting, she eagerly embraced whatever fate had in store for her.

His hand moved down her back, curved over her bottom and pressed her against his fierce arousal. Needing desperately to be even closer, to put out the fire that was blazing out of control, she pressed back, moving against him.

They both heard the whimper at the same time. Jax lifted his head, his eyes oddly unfocused.

''Sunny,'' she whispered.

"Probably just the rain."

Whatever it was, it was enough to put out the fire, or at least dampen it enough for Hetty to come to her senses. If she backed out now, she would always wonder what she'd missed, but wondering was better than regretting. Come tomorrow or next week or even the week after, he would buy her a ticket home and that would be the end of that.

"Hetty?"

The question lay unspoken between them.

"No. I don't think so. Jax, our worlds are so different. You're far more experienced than I ever will be. Gus was my only lover, and I knew him practically all my life."

"That doesn't mean—"

"It means that I can't afford to be in love with you, and if we make love, I might lose my perspective, and you see, I have to go home. I have to live with myself the rest of my life, and I'd as soon not make any more mistakes than I already have."

He didn't give away a single clue as to what he was thinking. It must be a lawyer thing, she told herself. She had no way of knowing if he was disappointed or relieved or merely bored.

"Yes, well—I'm glad we agree," she said gruffly in response to his silence. "Now I'd better go see if Sunny's kicked off her covers yet. And, uh, thank you for the supper. And the clothes. I—well, I suppose I'll see you tomorrow."

Seven

As it turned out, Hetty didn't see Jax until nearly eight the following evening. She was watching cable news when he let himself in, carrying his briefcase and a dark suit in a dry cleaner's bag. "I'll be going out pretty soon, so if you haven't eaten yet, order whatever you like for dinner. Why not try the seafood for a change?"

Dying of curiosity—she would never admit to disappointment—she nodded and said with admirable composure, "I think I'll have something light tonight. There's a good movie on TV at nine and I think Sunny might sleep through. She's certainly old enough."

She tried her best to concentrate on what was being

said about the explosive situation in the Middle East, but it was no good. She heard keys and change hit the dresser in the next room. Heard the soft thud of a shoe falling to the carpeted floor, then another one. A few moments later she heard the shower running. For the next several minutes she stared unseeingly at the moving figures on the TV screen while her imagination ran wild.

Some twenty minutes later Jax emerged, smelling of soap and a subtle, masculine scent, looking like an advertisement in one of those glossy fashion magazines.

"You look nice," she remarked. "Have a good time."

"Thanks, I'll try," he said as he removed a small, flat, silver-wrapped box from his briefcase and slipped it into his pocket. "Call Lina if you need to reach me, she'll know where I am."

She nodded, turning back to the TV as if she were really interested in whatever it was they were advertising. Lawn tractors. She didn't even have a lawn.

She didn't have a life, either, but she fully intended to get herself one. First a job, then an affordable apartment within walking distance of her old home. Because she did have a family, whether or not they were ready to accept her.

Jax obviously had a life. He had friends, social obligations, probably a whole string of gorgeous women panting after him. Just because he'd picked her up at an airport and brought her home with him like a stray cat—just because he'd kissed her a few times, didn't mean anything.

Besides, he really wasn't all that special, she told herself. None of his features was perfect. For one thing, his jaw was too strong. His nose was arched in a way that could only be called proud. His mouth was too wide, his eyes too deep-set, his—

Face it. The sum total of all his imperfections was nothing short of devastating. And unfortunately, Hetty admitted dolefully, she was in real danger of being devastated.

In a fashionable French restaurant across town, long, square-tipped fingers drummed on the table. For the third time since Faye had excused herself from the table to go powder her nose, Jax glanced at his watch. Once again he asked himself the same three questions he'd been silently asking all night.

What did I ever see in this woman?

How am I going to get out of this mess without hurting her feelings?

What is Hetty doing at this very moment?

By now she was probably wearing that oversize bathrobe, curled up in the rose-colored chair, watching her movie. Or maybe asleep with a book on her lap.

Unbidden, her image drifted before his imagination and lingered there like a half-remembered dream until the shrill sound of Faye's laughter reached him from several tables away. He flinched. His head ached.

Lately he'd been wondering if he needed reading glasses.

Welcome to middle age, he thought wryly. What went next, his hair? His joints? His prostate?

Across the room Faye leaned over to show off her new bracelet and, incidentally, a large slice of cleavage, to a well-dressed party of four at another table. He probably should've given her something nicer for her birthday, even though he intended to break things off as soon as he tactfully could. A box of candy would've been safer, but then, she'd have been disappointed after all the hints she'd dropped. Maybe a fountain pen set? Or a book?

Jax would be the first to admit that for a guy who'd graduated from law school third in his class, his I.Q. was about equal to his collar size when it came to women. It was going to take some pretty fancy maneuvering to extract himself from this particular relationship with no damage to Faye's ego.

"Hi, love, sorry to be gone so long, but I saw Harry and Reid and just had to say hello. They invited us to join their table, but I told them maybe later. They're drinking Dom Perignon."

"Would you like to join their party?"

"Would you?" Twisting in her chair, she wiggled her fingers at the party of three men and a woman, then turned back. "Is there any more champagne?"

More wine was the last thing she needed at this point. Fortunately—or unfortunately—she was one of those women who could drink and never pay the price. Tomorrow she'd be back in court bright and early, both her mind and her legal fangs razor sharp.

It made him feel old. "It's pretty late. I expect you're tired," he said diplomatically, swallowing a yawn. It was one of his more useful social skills.

"It's barely midnight. I thought we might go dancing, but of course, if you're not up to it…"

She was fresh out of law school. He felt older than granite. "You're the birthday girl."

So he drove them to her favorite club and they danced. On a dance floor he was adequate, no more, but he held her and moved to the music, pretending to an enthusiasm he no longer felt. If he ever had.

"I adore my bracelet. How did you know I love diamonds?"

Only because she'd mentioned it a few dozen times since he'd offered her a birthday dinner. "I don't know, just a lucky guess, I suppose."

Between dances, Faye hit the champagne. The bubbly, as she called it. Jax cringed every time she said the word. By the time they were ready to leave, his head was throbbing, and Faye was teetering on her skyscraper heels. She suggested a nightcap, her euphemism for sex. Most of their outings had ended that way for the past few months. But she was too tipsy, and he was too sober, and so he made his excuses and left, feeling both relieved and irritated for no reason he could put his finger on.

It was nearly 2:00 a.m. when he let himself into the suite. He could have gone to his own apartment as easily. This time of night he could have made it in under twenty minutes, but for reasons he dared not examine too closely, he chose to return to the hotel, letting himself inside quietly in deference to the late hour.

Hetty was asleep in a chair, the *Virginian Pilot* scattered around her feet, half a cup of curdled chocolate on the table beside her. Face scrubbed, hair tousled, she looked about fifteen instead of the thirty-seven he knew her to be.

Topcoat over his arm, tie dangling loosely about his neck, Jax stood for several minutes and stared. Exactly when, he wondered, not for the first time, had his life gone on the skids? When he'd first met Carolyn at the San Diego conference? When she'd called with the news that he was a father? When he'd gazed down for the first time at the small, solemn face of his own daughter?

Or when he'd turned around in the middle of a mob scene in a Chicago airport and found himself staring into a pair of calm, clear, rainwater-gray eyes?

Hetty.

If he'd had a grain of sense he would have avoided her like the plague, but at the time he'd needed her. And she had needed him. One thing had led to another, and now, whether or not he wanted it, she was a part of his life. An increasingly important part of it.

Stroking his shadowed jaw, he wondered if she was here solely because of his daughter or because she'd had no other choice, and he wondered if he'd played any part in her decision.

Better not to know. Safer not to know, he told himself.

Jax had nursed a single glass of champagne all evening, partly because he never drank and drove, but mostly because he hadn't felt like celebrating. After a hectic week he was running on fumes, which probably explained why his thoughts had a tendency to veer off onto paths best left unexplored.

The hotel felt airless compared to the cold, sea-scented air outside. He needed to get her out of here, into someplace more comfortable. Someplace more permanent.

Moving quietly, he tossed his topcoat on the sofa, shed his jacket and tie and removed his cuff links.

Hetty never stirred. Watching her, he felt a warmth begin to generate in the middle of his gut. He wasn't one of those people Streisand had sung about—the ones who needed people. Never had been.

Yet he couldn't deny feeling a sense of satisfaction in knowing she'd waited up for him. It was a first. To his knowledge no one had ever given a damn whether he came home or not.

As if sensing his presence, she stirred, yawned and sat up. Seeing him, she smiled, and if he wanted to pretend there was a degree of relief or welcome in her smile, what difference could it make?

"Sunny give you any trouble tonight?" He kept his voice low, just above a whisper.

"Not really. Just when I was convinced she was ready to sleep through the night, she woke up wanting to play. I guess it's because everything is still so new to her, she doesn't feel secure yet. I just settled her down again a few minutes ago.''

"Oh."

So she wasn't waiting up for him. Dammit, that was *not* disappointment he felt, it was heartburn! French cooking never had agreed with him.

Neither did complicated relationships with the opposite sex, he reminded himself. And with Hetty, any relationship at all would be complex. For all her lack of sophistication, she was not a simple woman.

Giving her time to get herself to bed, he went into his own room and changed into a pair of khakis, a sweatshirt and a pair of paint-stained deck shoes, all the while thinking about the woman in the next room.

As illogical as it was, he couldn't remember ever wanting a woman as much as he wanted Hetty Reynolds. It didn't make sense. He'd known far prettier women who hadn't affected him at all.

Besides, he'd already slept with her, if sleeping together on a hard, public floor, feeling her softness, her surprising strength and inhaling the arousing scent of her skin unadorned by any fancy perfume counted for anything.

Holding her in his arms with Sunny beside them in her carrier had been a memorable experience, one he was having trouble putting behind him. Evidently it had set off some kind of allergic reaction, because lately, all it took was a smile, a word, a touch, and he was primed and ready. If this was a midlife crisis, it was a damned awkward one.

Jax knew himself too well. He was genetically incapable of forming a permanent bond. Ever since he'd realized at the age of six that his mother wasn't coming back for him, the belief had taken root in his mind and grown there. Nothing had happened since then to change his mind. From the great-uncle who had grudgingly seen to his education, to his first love—she'd been seventeen to his fourteen—to any of the women since then with whom he'd formed temporary alliances.

He was not a family man. Adjusting to being a father was going to be enough of a challenge without adding to the complications. He was determined to be a father, and a damned good one, but he knew better than to risk trying to be anything more.

Hetty deserved more than he could offer. Judging from the few things she'd said, her marriage had been a good one. The stepfamily and in-laws had been a drag, but he knew her well enough by now to believe she wouldn't have seen them that way. When it came to nurturing a family, she was a natural.

When it came to nurturing anything more personal than a law firm, he was a nonstarter.

Silently he entered the living room, half expecting her to be gone. She was still there, her face flushed with sleep, her eyes glowing with that soft, unfocused look of the newly awakened.

"Go to bed," he said gruffly.

"I'm waiting to see if she's going to tune up again."

"Go to bed, if she wakes up I'll take care of her."

"There's coffee made if you want some," she murmured. One cheek was flushed where it had rested on her arm. Her hair stood up like a rooster's comb. She looked so warm, so sweet, so damned sexy, Jax had to remind himself all over again that while some men could handle a serious relationship with a woman, others were better off not trying.

He was of the latter persuasion.

"Go to bed, Hetty. I'll have a cup of coffee and then turn in."

She stretched one more time and yawned. "Mmm, I reckon I'd better. She'll be up with the chickens."

"I doubt it. It's been years since anyone saw a live chicken in downtown Norfolk."

She smiled at him, and he felt his defenses begin to crumble all over again. "Well…I guess I'd better say good-night." She seemed reluctant to go. He almost made the mistake of asking if she'd like a late-night snack when she said, "Jax, you look awfully tired."

"Yeah, I'm really bushed. I left a call for seven. I'll have breakfast downstairs so I won't wake you."

"I'll probably be up."

"Sleep as late as you can," he said, unwilling to let her go, calling himself every kind of fool for prolonging the agony. Pretty soon just looking at her wouldn't be enough, he would need to touch her, to hold her.

And then holding her would no longer be enough.

"Go to bed, Hetty," he growled.

Hetty had just fallen asleep when the alarm went off. It took her half a minute to realize what it was.

Not an alarm clock, but a steady clang, clang, clang.

Someone was shaking her awake. Clad only in a pair of briefs, Jax turned and scooped the baby out of her crib, grabbed a blanket off the bed and one from the crib and yelled, "Come on!"

Once she realized what was happening, Hetty wasted no time. Holding Sunny in one arm, Jax steered them out into the hall where the clamor was even more deafening.

All up and down the hallway, people were emerging from doorways, looking frightened, puzzled. They quickly became a mob and rushed toward the elevators, but Jax yelled, "Take the stairs!" Such was the authority he projected, even wearing only his briefs, that the swarm veered toward the stairwell, sweeping Hetty in their wake. One of the first things Jax had done when they'd checked into the room was study the diagram on the back of the door and show her where the nearest exit was. "Count the doors between our rooms and the exit," he'd told her, and she had, and then promptly forgotten the count.

Fortunately the lights were still on. There was no smell of smoke yet, but the noise was terrifying.

Holding Sunny in one arm, Jax held the heavy metal door open, took the arm of an elderly woman and handed her over to a young man wearing a ponytail and a single earring, then grabbed Hetty's hand and followed the crowd down the stairs. Not until they were halfway down the stairs did he take the time to drape the spare blanket over Hetty's shoulders.

She tucked the crib blanket around Sunny and asked, "What about you?" Her teeth were chattering, more from fear than from the cold.

"Warm-natured, remember?" He herded them down flight after flight. Once outside, he found a sheltered place out of the damp wind, away from the building, and held the two of them close. Through narrowed eyes he scanned the empty street beyond the huddled crowd for a sign of emergency traffic.

A taxi crawled past, and then a delivery van.

"What happened, does anyone know yet?" Other than a slight breathlessness, Hetty sounded as if this were no more than a fire drill. He hoped to God she was right, but he wasn't about to take any chances.

There were perhaps two dozen people outside this particular exit, with a few more straggling out from time to time. The murmur of voices grew louder as curiosity and outrage began to replace shock and fear. Someone said it was probably a kitchen fire. "Nine times outta ten, that's where they start. My son-in-law's got this boarding house. Some nut's always burning up popcorn in the microwave, setting off the smoke alarm."

Someone else mentioned laundry rooms. "Lint traps, there's your problem."

Still another man said it was probably a false alarm. Jax was inclined to agree. Nevertheless, he held his two ladies close and murmured words meant to be reassuring. "We'll know something pretty soon. Meanwhile, be glad the rain's let up for the moment."

Still no fire engines. Nothing but the incessant clanging of the alarm, which sounded somewhat muffled from where they had gathered. A few stragglers emerged through the double doors to join the group knotted around the garbage bins.

"Did you remember to bring our room key?" Hetty asked. She was standing storklike on one foot, the other drawn up under the trailing blanket. He wished he'd taken time to grab a pair of shoes.

"Feel around inside Sunny's sleeper. I didn't have a pocket."

"I would never have noticed," she said dryly. They shared a quick gleam of amusement.

A solitary police car rolled up and came to a stop. Jax handed over the baby and said, "Back in a minute, stay put." Then he jogged over to meet the officer.

From her sheltered location, Hetty watched the two men talk. The rain started up again, then stopped. It was cold. Jax was practically naked. There should be something ludicrous about a man wearing only rain-drenched briefs standing in the middle of the street, in the middle of the night.

Jax managed to looked heroic.

Once the shock of the emergency passed, he'd be frozen.

He could at least have grabbed a pair of shoes. She remembered how, back at the airport, he was forever slipping them off and then losing them in a space barely big enough to lie down in. Gus used to misplace things, too. His keys. His glasses. She hadn't thought anything of it. But with Jax's steel-trap mind, it was so out of character she found it endearing.

She was beginning to find entirely too many things about the man endearing.

"What are you smiling about? This is your idea of entertainment?" He appeared at her side while she was watching the ponytailed boy trying to cover the old woman's head with a newspaper.

"That's not a smile, it's a grimace. I'm freezing!"

"Next time, sleep in something warmer than that thing you're wearing."

"Look who's talking," she jeered, but when he drew her against his rain-drenched body she went willingly, wanting to share what little body heat she possessed.

Sunny started to bounce in her arms. "Oh, Lordy, she thinks it's time to wake up and play."

Jax lifted her into his own arms. "Great timing, kid. We'll never get you to sleep after this." He covered them as much as possible with the blanket.

Hetty asked what the officer had said, and Jax repeated the brief conversation. "He's gone inside to check it out, but so far it looks like a false alarm. We should know something in a few minutes."

"Before or after we turn into blocks of ice?" She tried to make light of it, but her feet had gone beyond hurting to numbness. Most of the people gathered outside were wearing robes and slippers. A few were fully dressed. Several of the women carried jewelry cases, one a hair dryer.

Hetty had left the bathrobe in the bathroom, and her new shoes were somewhere under the bed. With so little else to lose, other than her life, she hadn't taken time to grab anything. How many times could a woman lose everything she possessed?

She was still wondering when a man carrying a flashlight rounded the corner and hurried toward where the small group was huddled. He was wearing a doorman's braid-trimmed topcoat over striped pajamas. "Sorry for the trouble, folks. New computerized security system. Either Y2K struck again or somebody hit the wrong button. Y'all can go back inside now. Manager said to tell you there'll be an adjustment on your bills."

Hetty looked to Jax for confirmation. "That's it? All this excitement and we're supposed to go back inside as if it had never happened?"

"You want to stand outside and argue?"

"Who, me? I'm too cold to argue."

"I'll keep that in mind," he said, steering them back inside. The temperature was only in the forties, but the windchill was definitely a factor.

By the time he retrieved the room key from the foot of Sunny's sleeper and let them inside the suite, Hetty's teeth were chattering audibly. His own metabolism was such that he adjusted to the cold pretty well, and Sunny seemed none the worse for the exposure, if her two-tooth grin was any indication. The kid obviously thrived on excitement.

He felt her bottom like an old pro, then carried her to the crib. "Go run a tub of hot water and jump in," he called over his shoulder.

"I've already used a week's worth of hot water."

"Use my tub, then. Or climb back in bed and cover up."

"I'm too keyed-up to sleep. Maybe some hot chocolate? Is it too late for room service?"

"They're probably about ready to start on breakfast. Sun'll be up in a couple of hours."

Arms wrapped around her, she was standing in her bedroom doorway, one bare foot covering the other, waiting to see if Sunny was going to settle. "I could make coffee." She was shivering so hard the words were barely intelligible.

"Coffee won't help you sleep."

Jax tilted his head to listen, then crossed the room and pulled the bedroom door shut. "She's down and out."

"I can't believe it. She seems to thrive on excitement."

"You're still cold, aren't you?" Shaking his head, Jax opened his arms and said, "Take off that wet blanket, then come here and let me warm you up before you shake your joints loose."

"I really shouldn't," she said. Then, letting the blanket fall to the floor, she walked into his warm embrace.

"Between us, we ought to be able to generate a little steam heat."

She laughed softly, then tucked her cold hands under his arms. "May I? A lady doesn't like to presume."

"A lady ought to know better than to sleep in a thin T-shirt in this kind of weather. As soon as the stores open I want you to go buy yourself several pairs of flannel pajamas."

"And some hunting socks. I used to sleep in Gus's hunting socks when it got real cold. My feet are like blocks of ice." She slid her toes up the calf of his leg, and he laughed, but it was a shaky effort.

"Come on, I'll let you borrow my sweatshirt."

They never even made it to the chair where he'd left his clothes. Somehow—afterward Hetty was never quite sure how it happened—they ended up in Jax's bed with her cold feet clutched between his big warm ones, her cold body plastered against his heated flesh. "Better?" he murmured.

By that time she couldn't have spoken if her life depended on it. The feelings that had started when her breasts had been crushed against his chest quickly turned into a pleasure so intense it was almost pain.

A need so deep it blinded her to all reason.

Hetty knew what was going to happen. They both knew. And because she wanted his kiss, wanted whatever he could give her, wanted so desperately to follow this fierce compulsion to its inevitable conclusion, she lifted her face eagerly when he came searching for her mouth.

His hands moved to cover her breasts, causing her nipples to harden and push against his palms. Lowering his mouth, he suckled her there, drawing forth a soft cry from her lips.

She thought he whispered her name, but the words were lost as he began to roll up her damp knit shirt. Hetty tugged at his briefs, boldly, shamelessly taking the lead for the first time in her life. In the early days of her marriage she'd been tempted. She'd found herself wanting to experiment, but embarrassed to suggest trying something new. Gus had had his own routine when it came to sex. When it came to almost everything. He'd been a methodical man. A safe, dependable man. It was one of the things she'd loved about him.

There was nothing at all safe or routine about what was happening to her now. It was if a stranger had been hiding inside her all these years, a hungry, shameless creature who made demands, who followed instincts that Hetty had never dreamed she possessed, one who felt pleasure beyond her wildest imagination.

Even more surprising, she was no silent lover. Amazed, she heard herself repeating his name again and again, begging shamelessly for his touch, for his kisses in places where she ached to feel them.

Jax felt her hands moving over his body, lingering on his chest, her fingertips brushing over his flat nipples, causing them to harden instantly. He groaned as her lips took their place. "Is this all right?" she whispered.

"It's all right." His voice grated harshly in the silent room. He groaned again when her hands skimmed down his body, following the trail of coarse dark hair that led to his throbbing sex.

She was incredible. For a woman who'd been married all those years, she was surprisingly awkward. Bold, yet oddly hesitant. "Sweetheart, I can't hold back much longer." His turgid flesh leaped as he felt the brush of her fingers, felt them close around him. "Ahh, Hetty, wait—let me—"

He wanted to make it last. To make it good for her. Better than good, unforgettable. But by the time he mounted her he was long past any semblance of control. The moment he felt her silken thighs close around his hips he plunged, withdrew slowly and plunged again. Holding his breath, he struggled to regain control, but it was too late. His head thrown back, eyes tightly closed, he shuddered, thrust quickly once more, then cried out his release.

Eons later, when he could find the strength, he lifted his head from her shoulder. "Ahh, Hetty, I'm sorry. You didn't...did you?" He should've been able to tell, but it had taken him by surprise. The sheer power of it. No other woman had ever driven him so quickly, so completely, over the edge. He could only apologize.

"I'm not sure," she said thoughtfully, her breath still coming in throbbing little gasps.

"Hetty?" He rolled over onto his side, carrying her with him. Sliding his hand between their damp bodies, he found her, heard the quick intake of her breath and knew beyond any doubt that she was still hovering on the edge of fulfillment.

A touch was all it took. A single caress, and she stiffened in his arms, gave one deep, shuddering gasp, then collapsed.

Some time later, when her breath and his had slowed to normal levels, he started to speak, realized he had no idea what to say, and thought that, all things considered, it might be better to say nothing.

Silently he thought about the possible consequences of one rash act. Only a few feet away, sleeping peacefully in the next room, was the consequence of another such a lapse in judgment.

He might be a fool. He was no coward.

"Hetty, if you—are you—that is, I didn't use anything."

"I know. I'm safe. That is, I've never—well, you know. Since Gus, I mean. Before him, either, for that matter. I guess it showed—that I'm not terribly experienced, I mean, and as for the other, I've always been regular, and I know they say it's not foolproof, but in my case, it must be, because I never got pregnant. So you don't have to…"

He tucked her face into his throat, wondering whether to laugh or cry. How many ways could a man mess up his life?

He was beginning to suspect that his own was deeply screwed up.

"I know all about—well, everything. I've read lots of articles, and you hear about it in the news all the time, and I can understand why you're—"

"Hetty. You're babbling again."

"I know. I warned you I tend to do that whenever—"

"You feel nervous. Yeah, I remember."

She took a deep breath and began to pull away. Jax held on, unwilling to let her go because she felt so good, so right in his bed, in his arms.

And because...

"Hetty," he whispered against her ear.

That was all it took.

Jax opened his eyes a few hours later, sensing another body in the bed beside him. Orientation was not a problem. Instant recall was both a curse and a blessing. He lay there, arms crossed under his head, and thought about what had happened.

Happened not once, not twice, but three times!

It was damned near a miracle.

Reserved by nature, Jax was not a man to lose his head over sex. He'd always considered himself an adequate lover. Cautious, sensible, but generous.

With Hetty he'd become a raging stud.

Rolling over onto his side, he gazed down at the sleeping woman beside him. Her breathing was deep and steady, her eyelids not even quivering.

She was smiling.

Eight

It was Lina who moved Hetty and the baby into a small apartment. "It's my niece's place, but she's out of the country for the next three weeks. By then Jax will have found something else."

And someone else, Hetty thought, but didn't say so.

"She won't mind? Your niece?"

"Goodness, no. She'd do anything for Jax. Had a crush on him since the first time she met him, when she was still in high school."

"Yes, well...we won't touch anything."

"Touch all you want. Another few weeks and you won't be able to keep that baby out of mischief, though. I'd put things up out of her reach if I were you."

Hetty did. She unpacked and set up the playpen and the crib she'd bought with Lina's help. The stroller and carrier she placed by the door for convenience.

Jax seemed in no hurry to visit their new quarters. In fact, Hetty hadn't heard from him since the night they had made love. He'd been gone when she'd woken up that morning. Evidently he was as embarrassed by the whole thing as she was, although she couldn't think why. She was the one who had acted so shamelessly. She'd actually begged him to do it again and again.

She blew upward in an attempt to cool her flaming face. Even now she couldn't believe she had done the things she had done, said the things she had said—actually begged him to—

Well. Enough about that. It was time to plant her feet firmly back on the earth, and the first thing she would do was to call Jeannie. If she didn't get through, she would write. Surely Nicky wouldn't hide her mail. He was spiteful, but it was mostly because he was immature and unsure of himself. Eighteen was pretty young to be a father, a husband and a home-owner.

She waited until after Sunny went down for her nap to place the call, hoping that Nicky would be out. Hoping he'd found a job by now.

''Jeannie? It's me, Hetty. I just wanted to let you know—''

But before she could let her know anything, she had to listen while her stepdaughter complained about the cost of baby-sitters and the cost of owning a home.

"Does having to fill out that thing that came from the tax office mean I have to pay house taxes?"

Hetty admitted that it meant just that. She said, "I know, honey, it's tough at the moment, but if Nicky can find a good job—yes, I'm sure he has, but—well, of course he is—no, I can't come home right away, I have a—"

Hetty's shoulders sagged. "How's Robert? Did you take him for his six-month checkup?"

And then she was forced to listen to a recital of how expensive taking care of a baby was, with diapers and pediatricians's bills and baby food. That was followed by a few snide remarks about people who could afford to go off on cruises while other people had to stay home and work. "It was Daddy's insurance money. I don't see why you had to keep it all."

Hetty didn't bother to remind her that most of Gus's small insurance settlement had gone to pay Sadie's medical and burial expenses, the household living expenses, plus the bills Jeannie had run up before she'd run off. After that there had been Robert.

She said only, "I know babies can be expensive, honey, but they're worth every penny and every minute you spend on them."

Not until after she hung up did she realize that she had neither asked to come home nor promised to. Nor had she mentioned her own penniless state. Replacing the phone, she sat for several minutes, feeling a mixture of guilt and relief. At least she knew now that

Jeannie would welcome her back. She suspected even Nicky would be willing to put up with her as long as she agreed to pay room and board and take over Robert's care while they both worked.

Although how he expected her to earn enough to pay room and board, and at the same time take care of Robert, was beyond her.

They would just have to learn the facts of life, Hetty told herself. She had done it. There was something to be said for the sink-or-swim method of gaining an education.

On the bright side, maybe things weren't quite so hopeless as she'd thought. True, she had missed her cruise, which meant she had wasted an awful lot of money. On the other hand, she'd had herself an affair, which she would never have dreamed of doing back home, even if there'd been anyone she was faintly interested in.

She had seen places she had never expected to see. She had always dreamed of traveling, and now she had. There was nothing to keep her from going back home, settling down in her comfortable, familiar rut and taking care of Robert while his parents finished growing up.

Oddly enough, the prospect didn't seem nearly as inviting as it would have only a few days ago.

Jax put it off as long as he could, two days, to be exact, but in the end he drove across town to the address Lina had given him, where Hetty and Sunny were staying.

He should have called first. They might not even be there. On a day like this, the first in nearly a week without the threat of rain, Hetty had probably cranked up the new stroller and gone out to explore.

He only hoped the place was in a decent neighborhood. Lina had vouched for it, and he trusted his secretary implicitly.

Which meant there were now two women he trusted. That was a record. He'd have to watch his step or risk losing his cynicism. For a man in his profession, that could be a real handicap.

The apartment was in one of the older homes near the college that had been turned into student housing. It was no worse than most, but no better. He needed to settle on a house as quickly as possible, and get them moved in.

The foyer smelled of stale pizza, cigarette smoke, incense and room freshener. Trying not to inhale too deeply, he climbed the stairs. By the time he reached the second floor and thumbed the buzzer, he was frowning. The stairs were both steep and narrow. To go out, Hetty would have to wrestle the stroller down to the first floor, then go back and get Sunny. Not an ideal situation.

"Jax! I—I wasn't expecting you."

"Those stairs are a hazard."

"The stairs?"

"Maybe I should have called first, but— Are you busy?"

She was even more beautiful than he remembered, despite the wet towel tied around her waist and the wriggling baby under her arm. He told himself to back off and start again before she slammed the door in his face.

So he did. "Hi, sweetheart," he greeted his daughter, taking one small bare foot in his hand. "Hey, she's smiling. You think she recognizes me?"

"Of course she recognizes you, you're her father. Come in and let me close the door, we're letting the heat out."

Feeling awkward, he stood until she told him for heaven's sake, to sit down. "You take up too much room, standing in the middle of the floor."

The place was small, all right. The word *cramped* came to mind. There was the usual student furniture, including a plank-and-cement-block bookcase, a yardsale sofa and chair and a mismatched dining set.

"So—I see you got settled in all right." Go ahead, impress her with your conversational skills, why don't you?

"Lina took care of everything, the hotel bill and all. She let me stop off at a supermarket, since eating out with a baby can be awkward."

"What about takeout? Here, let me—" He reached for his wallet.

"No." They'd argued over her salary, with Hetty insisting she didn't want to be paid in advance, it was too much like being in debt. "Lina bought the groceries. She put them on your credit card, so everything's all taken care of. There's a two-burner surface unit and a tiny refrigerator, and we manage just fine, don't we, sugar?"

Sunny responded by starting to fuss. "I'd better finish getting her dressed."

Frustrated on several accounts, Jax watched her disappear into the bedroom. He wondered if she was as embarrassed as he was, and for the same reason. It was the first time they'd been together since the night they'd made love. He'd left before she'd woken up the next morning, telling himself he needed time to go home, shower and shave before going to the office. But the truth was, he'd awakened with some crazy notion of making an honest woman of her. It had scared the hell out of him, so he'd run.

Swearing silently, he crossed to the window, a matter of three paces across an ugly fake Oriental rug. Staring down at the passing traffic, he told himself that what he ought to do was follow her into the bedroom and settle this thing once and for all.

Only he would probably end up getting in even deeper. For a guy who was supposed to be reasonably intelligent, he was making one damn-fool mistake after another. Not only socially, but legally.

Technically Hetty was his employee. He didn't think of her that way, but technically that's exactly what she was. The only reason he hadn't paid her a month's salary in advance was that she refused to take it. For the sake of her prickly pride they'd settled on some sort of barter system. She looked after his daughter full-time, and he paid all her living expenses. She'd swallowed it, but not willingly.

But no matter how you sliced it, the woman was his employee, and he had seduced her. Which cast what had happened into a totally different light. Being a lawyer, he could hardly ignore that aspect.

Abruptly he turned and was about to march into the bedroom with some notion of getting everything out into the open, when she slipped back through the door, pulling it almost shut behind her.

"There—she should play for a little while. I bought her some crib toys, I hope you don't mind. When she gets tired of playing we'll have milk and bananas and she'll help me fix supper."

It took the wind clean out of his sails. Jax stared at her, wondering how she could be so calm, when he was so damned conflicted. From wanting her, to exposing himself to harassment charges, back to wanting her in a way that was painfully obvious.

Hadn't she even noticed? Could she possibly be all that indifferent? Was he the only one involved here?

Oh, hell. "I'd better go," he said abruptly. "I just thought I'd come by and see Sunny, but since she's asleep—"

"Jax—"

"I'll be looking at houses again tomorrow, so I might not have time to—"

"Jax?"

"And interviewing. I'll get Lina to set up some interviews with—"

"Jackson!"

"What!"

She shook her head slowly. "Listen to us, we're yelling at each other. I can't think of a single reason why we should. I thought we'd parted friends, at least."

He raked his fingers through his hair, then dropped down onto one of the red-enameled kitchen chairs. "Yeah, you're right. I guess I'm still off balance. This sort of thing is new to me."

"Being a father? Buying a house?"

He glared at her. "You know what I'm talking about. Hetty, believe it or not, I'm not used to spending a night in a woman's bed and then having to deal with her on another level. I've always kept my—my social life and my professional life in different compartments. What am I supposed to say? Do we talk about your work, or do we talk about—" he shrugged "—about other things?"

Hetty studied him for several moments, wondering how any man could look so arrogant and so vulnerable at the same time. It was part of his charm, she supposed—looking the way he did and being the way he was.

Which to her way of thinking was about as close to perfect as any man could be.

"We don't have to talk at all if you'd rather not. Now that we've—well, we've got the personal matter out of our systems, we can—"

"Personal matter! Is that what you call it? And what do you mean, we've got it out of our systems?"

Her voice grew even quieter in contrast to his own belligerence. "I only meant now we can get on with the business of finding you someone to look after Sunny." He started to interrupt her again, but she held up a hand. "Jax, would you let me—that is, I'd like to help you interview nannies. Sometimes a woman's point of view can be helpful."

"A woman's point of view? You mean like that book about martians?"

She knew exactly which book he meant, because the library had given in to popular demand and acquired the bestseller that had compared men to the planet Mars and women to the planet Venus.

She shrugged. "Whatever you want to call it, you have to admit that you don't have much experience in dealing with babies."

"And you do, I suppose. Got a degree in infant and child development." He was being a jerk, and he knew it.

"No, but I've been a daughter, a stepmother, and a stepgrandmother. I kept Robert until he was almost Sunny's age. That should count for something. I do know that Sunny will adjust better with someone who won't try to force her into a strict schedule. Babies need structure, but she'll set her own routine soon enough."

So it was decided. Nothing else was. Jax left a few minutes later feeling more conflicted than ever. He'd wanted to haul her into his arms and kiss the living daylights out of her, then take her into that closet-size bedroom and make love to her until he lacked the strength to fall out of bed.

But he hadn't. Thank God he wasn't entirely brain dead yet.

The real estate saleswoman had left word that she had a couple of places she would like to show him and would he be available the following day?

Lina said, "You're meeting her at this address tomorrow at two. I've postponed Henderson until Thursday. He was glad of the extra time, because it gives him a chance to get together with the liability people."

"How about calling that temp place you were telling me about and seeing what you can set up for today. After five, preferably. You know what I'll be needing."

Lina gave him what he thought of as her drill sergeant look. "I know what you're needing, all right, and it's not another one of those antacid pills you keep chewing on. Those things might make your bones stronger, but your stomach's not going to settle until you face up to certain facts."

He didn't ask what facts, because he didn't want to know. Some facts were best avoided as long as possible.

"I made you an appointment with an ophthalmologist for next week. Men and their silly pride." She shook her head. "You're starting to get squint lines."

He called Hetty and told her about the interviews Lina had set up. "We're meeting in my office this afternoon after work. If it's all right with you, I can pick you up at four-thirty."

"We'll be ready."

"We?"

"Sunny and I."

He said, "Oh, yeah," hung up the phone and smacked himself on the forehead with his fist. It had been that kind of day. Tomorrow didn't promise to be any better, what with the feds trying to pin down the ship owner about paying for the cleanup, the captain responsible for the spill in the hospital with a ruptured appendix and an appointment to look at houses.

As if he knew the first thing about looking at houses.

With all that on his mind, he kept imagining himself asking Hetty things like, "King-size or queen-size, honey? I think a queen-size bed's big enough, don't you?"

Things like, "Gas logs or the real thing? Me, I kind of fancy sitting in front of a real log fire, don't you?"

As though they'd be sharing everything.

"Lady, you are seriously screwing up my brain," he muttered as he cleared his desk of the day's accumulation and slammed shut the top drawer.

She was ready when he arrived. Correction—they were ready. Sunny was wearing a new yellow snowsuit—did they still call them that? Kids had worn snowsuits when he was a boy. He couldn't remember much of his early childhood, but he remembered that much.

Hetty wore a dark skirt under an all-weather coat. Her shoes were the kind invariably described as "sensible."

On her they looked sexy as the devil.

"We've got rush-hour traffic to contend with. Lina

set up four interviews, with the first one set for six. We allowed twenty minutes for each, which means it might cut into dinnertime. Will twenty minutes each be long enough?''

"It sounds about right. I've never interviewed anyone before.''

"I thought you were the expert.'' He skillfully avoided a collision with a stalled delivery truck.

"Not on hiring, on babies. And I never claimed to be an expert.'' Sunny was in her carrier, strapped into the back seat. She was making noises. "Did you hear that?'' Hetty exclaimed, beaming. "She called you Daddy.''

"Sounded like doggy to me.''

"Who's the expert here?''

"Yes, ma'am. Duly noted.''

They were bantering, almost the way they had back at the airport once they'd gotten used to each other. As bad as things had been before they'd finally escaped, she had never lost her sense of humor.

Of the four applicants scheduled, the first was a no-show. "Reliability is important,'' Hetty said. "I guess showing up counts for something.''

"Might be stuck in traffic somewhere,'' Jax offered, feeling generous. They were in his pine-paneled office. Sunny was on his lap playing with a wad of rubber bands while Hetty admired the view of the shipyard from his corner window.

"I didn't realize we were this close to the water.''

"In Norfolk, you're never that far away. Although

at the rate it's growing, pretty soon Greater Norfolk will take in more territory than a few states I could mention.''

''Where do you keep your boat?''

''Little place on the Intracoastal Waterway. Sort of a mom and pop marina. I'll take you there this weekend and show you.''

''Oh, but—''

Before she could voice whatever excuse she'd been about to put forth, the next applicant showed up. She was chewing gum. She wore the kind of perfume that was priced by the pint instead of the ounce. All the same, Jax went through the process and promised to let her know by the next afternoon.

''Poor thing, she'll be disappointed,'' Hetty said after the woman had left, leaving her potent essence behind. ''She might really need the job.''

Jax opened a window and let the fresh air blow through for a few minutes. ''I haven't noticed a lack of Help Wanted signs lately, have you? She'll find something if she's really interested.''

''I hope so,'' Hetty murmured, looking worried as he called in the next applicant. Dammit, Jax told himself, there was such a thing as having too soft a heart.

The next woman had requirements of her own, including health insurance, two full days off a week, her own living quarters and a car at her disposal.

''Well, hell,'' Jax said plaintively after she'd been shown out. ''At this rate, I'm never going to find help.'' He raked his fingers through his hair, a habit he had when he was tired and worried and things weren't falling into a neat, orderly pattern.

"Those were reasonable requests. Maybe not the insurance—at least, not right off. All the same, someone a little more flexible might be better. With babies, you can never tell what might come up." Hetty was sitting across the room holding a drowsy Sunny on her lap, the baby's head pillowed on her breast.

Jax wished it were his head. He wished—

The next applicant, a red-cheeked young woman who didn't look old enough to be out of school, poked her head through the doorway and called out, "Hi, am I too late? Have you already found someone?"

So they went through the process all over again, and Jax told her they would let her know tomorrow.

Hetty, gathering up Sunny's diaper bag, her own purse and coat, said, "Now that one, I like."

"She's just a kid."

"She showed up. That means she's at least marginally responsible."

"Or hungry."

"So? She's bright and cheerful, and with babies that counts for a lot. Besides, she said she had seven brothers and sisters, so she's obviously had experience."

"So have you."

Hetty didn't know what to say to that, so she didn't say anything. Jax locked up and saw them out into the cold, damp air. "Is that ocean I smell?" she asked as he bundled them into the car.

"Yeah, I guess it is. It carries when the wind's out of the northeast."

He'd hardly noticed, having inhaled so deeply when he was reaching past her to fasten Sunny into her carrier that his head was still reeling. She smelled of her own clean, subtle fragrance. He suspected it was little more than soap, shampoo and hand lotion, plus her own particular chemistry.

Whatever it was, it affected his senses in a way no expensive perfume ever had.

He drove without attempting to make conversation. Traffic was still heavy. Sunny was humming. At least that was the only way he could describe it.

He glanced in the rearview mirror. "Is she okay?"

"She's fine. She'll be singing for her supper in a little while, though, so we'd better not waste time getting home."

Home. When was the last time he'd thought about home? There had been a series of boarding schools, the university, the marine corps, then law school. He'd lived in a series of dormitories, rooms and apartments, from the cheapest to the luxury kind where he lived now.

One thing there had never been—at least none that he could recall—was a place he called home.

"I thought we'd stop and get something to eat," he said.

"I could scramble us some eggs. Or maybe make an omelet."

"You're on," he said, hoping he wasn't going to make any more serious mistakes.

Nine

She could cook. She was a natural with babies. She looked delectable no matter what she was wearing—or not wearing. Her background and his were completely different. Not a single point of reference so far as he could tell. And yet…

And yet, despite the fact that his was a trained legal mind, Jax knew he was in serious danger of tossing out all the evidence, pro and con, and going on gut feeling alone.

Hetty scooped up a spoonful of eggs from Sunny's plate. "What about a combination? The woman with all the demands, Mrs. Charles, and—what was her name? The one with the large family?"

"Roselle McCarter."

"I'll bet they call her Rosie. Anyway, Rosie could come in on Mrs. Charles's days off and maybe fill in at other times, if she doesn't find anything better."

"Hmm?" Jax had been busy admiring the graceful movements of her hand as she poked food into Sunny's birdlike mouth. "Don't kids usually sit in high chairs?"

"She'll need one pretty soon, but until she's a little steadier on her bottom, the carrier on a chair works fine. Oops! No, not in your hair, honey." She caught the wad of eggs just before it could be massaged into Sunny's dark curls. "Her table manners need a bit of polishing, but she's learning, aren't you, sugar?"

Jax was entranced. It occurred to him that this was the sort of scene some men might find boring. Jax found it totally absorbing. But then, he could remember spending hours at the zoo, watching the mama apes holding, feeding and grooming their offspring.

Was this a part of what was called bonding? He'd never thought much about it before. He'd damn sure never bonded with anyone, child or adult.

"Hetty, how about checking out a couple of houses with me tomorrow? Unless you've got something else scheduled, that is."

"Well, we'd planned to find some water and look at boats. I told her about her great-great-however-many-greats-grandfather. The one who adopted the baby girl?"

"Oh, yeah, she'll be fascinated by her so-called heritage, I'm sure. Seriously, I wouldn't mind getting a woman's perspective."

She hesitated so long he thought she was going to refuse, but she nodded. "We'll be glad to offer an opinion for what it's worth, but when it comes to houses, my experience is pretty limited. You might want to ask someone else?"

It was another statement in the form of a question. He didn't know if it was an Oklahoma thing, or merely a sign of her insecurity. Then Sunny dropped a chunk of mashed banana onto the floor. Grateful for the distraction, he said, "I'll get it."

"No, let me." She swooped down and scooped up that and several wads of egg. No fool, he took advantage of it to admire the graceful line of her back when she leaned over. Her shirt and skirt parted to reveal a narrow view of white nylon slip, setting fire to his imagination.

You're losing it, Powers.

Once supper was over, he insisted on helping with his daughter's bed prep. The bath, the nuzzling, the diapering, the nuzzling, the fitting of small moving body parts into a flannel sleeper. More nuzzling. It seemed to be an important part of the process.

"I need to know how to do this stuff. She didn't come with instructions," he said.

"You'll do fine. Common sense, love and a few pointers is all you need."

Sunny, drowsy and flushed from her bath, grinned up at him, and he felt a physical pain in the region of his heart.

Hetty picked her up, buried her face in the plump,

sweet-smelling neck and made blowing noises. "I shouldn't do that," she said ruefully. "Now she's wide-awake."

While she settled the gurgling baby in the crib, Jax lingered, taking in the tableau of woman and child.

He cleared his throat. "We need to talk about transportation. If you're going to be able to get around, you'll need something to drive."

Backing away from the crib, Hetty switched off the lamp, leaving only the pink glow of a night-light. She waved him out and pulled the door almost closed. Then, turning to confront him, she said flatly, "No. Don't even think of it."

"What, you don't drive?"

"Of course I drive. I've been driving since I was thirteen, only not in strange cities where there's all this traffic and I don't know my way around. For as much time as I'll be here, it's hardly worth renting something."

He hadn't been planning to rent her a car, he'd planned to buy her one. Something small enough to be manageable, but big enough to be safe. He dismissed the idea of public transportation out of hand. Too much waiting around in cold, damp weather. "I'll get you a city map. Lina can take you out a few times and show you how to locate the closest shopping center, things like that."

"Thanks, but I don't think so."

He didn't argue. That didn't mean he'd given up, it only meant that his timing was off. He would wait a few days. "One of the houses we'll be checking out tomorrow is located on the Intracoastal Waterway, not far from where I keep my boat. I thought we'd save that one until last, and then I'll introduce you ladies to the *Lizzie-Linda*."

"I'd like that. A friend of mine has a bass boat he tows miles and miles to this fishing camp? He keeps inviting me to go fishing, but I've never had time."

She sounded wistful. As if she would have liked to go, and maybe not just for the fishing. He wondered who the jerk was, and told himself his boat was bigger than any flashy little freshwater outboard. "You understand, *Lizzie* isn't in the water yet—she still needs a lot of work, but she's going to be a real beauty once I get her back to her original condition. She's fifty-five foot eight with an eighteen-foot beam."

Her smile was the kind of smile that made him wonder if he was bragging too much. Come to think of it, it did sound pretty juvenile. The "mine's bigger than yours" syndrome.

"Want some coffee before you go?"

"No, thanks." What he wanted wasn't coffee or platitudes or even conversation. What he wanted was to wrap her in his arms and kiss her until neither of them had the strength to stand or the will to resist. And then he wanted to take her to bed and make love to her. Quick, hard love, followed by slow, sensuous love. And when they were both too exhausted to explore further, he wanted to hold her while she slept.

Help! Man overboard.

He collected his coat and turned toward the door.

Silently she watched him prepare to leave.

And then he turned back.

The apartment was small. Five steps and he was standing in front of her, so close he could feel her warmth, inhale the soap-and-lotion smell of her skin. Dropping his coat, he gathered her into his arms and buried his face in her hair.

"Don't ask me what's going on here, I'm damned if I know," he muttered against her ear. "The only thing I'm sure of is that if I don't kiss you right now, the sky's going to fall." He shot her a whimsical grin. "You don't want to be responsible for the collapse of the universe, do you?"

She shook her head, then nodded, then lifted her face to his. Their eyes met and held, and if he'd been conked on the head by a falling star, he wouldn't have noticed.

Slow and easy, a dim voice in the back of his mind cautioned. Don't try to grab more than she's ready to give.

He touched his parted lips to hers. Slow and easy lasted for all of five seconds, and then he groaned, twisted his head and thrust his tongue into the sweet warmth of her mouth. Fiercely, instantly aroused, he pressed his groin against her pelvic mound. Sweet, mind-numbing torment. Every brain cell he possessed was focused on the region just below his belt.

The kiss went as far as a kiss could possibly go. Farther. It wasn't enough. Without breaking contact, he tried to reach the buttons of her shirt, gave it up and cradled her breasts through layers of clothing. She pressed herself into his hands, whimpering against his mouth.

"Ah, sweet, sweet," he muttered incoherently against her lips. His shaking hands skimmed down her body, cradling her hips to hold her against him. It still wasn't enough, he had to get closer.

Broken thoughts raced through his mind like cloud shadows on a windy day, then he gave up trying to think. It was a clear sign of how far off course he'd strayed. Reason was his middle name. Reason, logic, caution were the rules he lived by.

"Sweetheart, do you think the bed—?" His voice sounded like tearing canvas.

"We'd wake the baby." Hers, like whispering silk.

"A blanket on the floor?" He couldn't stand the thought of her naked skin against that hideous fake Oriental rug.

"The sofa opens up into a double bed," she offered, coming to the rescue.

They managed to get the thing open. Jax prayed it wouldn't collapse under them. If it did, he doubted either of them would notice.

"Take off your—here, let me," he said at the same time Hetty began fumbling at the buttons on his shirt. Together they managed to undress, hands tangling in haste, breathless laughter interspersed with more kisses.

Intoxicated. He was drunk on lo—

On lust.

She was as eager as he was. They fell onto the bed in a tangle of limbs. Jax did his best to spare her his weight, but with Hetty reaching for him, pulling him down to rest between her thighs, there was no way he could hold off. She was ready for him. Warm, wet and wild. He entered her swiftly and then lay still while she twisted and writhed beneath him.

As a woman she was quiet, modest, sensible.

As a lover, she was totally uninhibited.

The last shred of control broke, and the race was on. Separately and together they hurtled toward the finish line. Time and space telescoped into one fiercely burning point of pleasure that swooped closer, closer...

The sound of harsh breathing. Gasping. Someone shouted—or maybe they both did—and then they collapsed together, all limp limbs and winded, damp bodies.

Jax felt as if he'd been caught by a storm surge and flung hard against a seawall. As soon as he could find the strength he rolled onto his side, carrying her with him. He refused to let her go.

He might never let her go.

They slept. How long, neither of them could have said, but the sound of a plaintive wail from the next room brought Hetty around. ''Oh, mercy, I forgot...''

''I'll do it,'' Jax muttered drowsily.

''Do what?'' Was that a note of regret he detected in her voice?

He opened his eyes. ''Do—whatever it is that needs doing.''

''Fine, then I'll take care of Sunny while you get

dressed. Have a shower first if you want to, but then you'd better leave.''

He blinked, sat up and raked his fingers through his hair. He wasn't ready to leave. Wasn't at all sure he could make it as far as her bathroom, much less down those steep, narrow stairs. ''I could stay over.''

''I'd rather you didn't,'' she said quietly, making him wonder if she was already regretting it. The last time they'd made love, he'd been the one to flee in panic. He'd stayed away for two days, afraid to come around again because he wasn't ready to talk about it, and women always wanted to talk things to death.

Hetty hadn't mentioned it at all. From the way she'd reacted when he finally showed up, you'd have thought they'd spent a quiet evening at the public library instead of making wild, passionate love.

She was stonewalling. He knew the signs. Watching her gather up her scattered clothes and disappear into the bedroom, he wanted to yell after her, ''What the hell is going on here?''

But he didn't. Trained legal mind. Too much pride. This time it was his pride, not hers. His fault for expecting too much. For expecting anything at all.

Dressing quickly, Jax made up his mind to hire the first halfway suitable candidate he could find to look after his daughter, and let Ms. Oklahoma go back where she belonged.

He was on his way out when Hetty opened the bedroom door. Her hair was a mess, her eyes were suspiciously glittery and there was a beard burn on the left side of her neck. ''Do you still want me to look at houses tomorrow?'' She obviously expected him to back out.

''Sure, why not?'' Two could play at this game. If she didn't care, then he didn't care twice as much!

It was one of those days sent to lend hope after a rugged winter. Late pansies, early forsythia and a few bold crocuses under a clear sky. Sunny wore her new yellow snowsuit. All strapped into her carrier, she grinned up at him, showing off the two pearly nubs on her lower gum.

Hetty was wearing the same drab all-weather coat. The thing was padded; she could have been built like a refrigerator and it wouldn't have shown.

There were shadows under her eyes.

There were shadows in her smile, but she said brightly, ''Sunny wants to announce another tooth is on the way.''

If that was the way she wanted to play it, then Jax was willing. More than willing. A messy relationship was something he could do without. ''I foresee a long line of dentist bills ahead.''

''Try the barter system. Find a good dentist and trade him legal advice for dental care.''

''Unless he has a boat, my legal services won't do him much good.''

''I thought lawyers were interchangeable. One size fits all.''

''Bite your tongue, lady. You think doctors are the only profession that specializes?''

They were back to bantering. That was fine with him. Keep it light, make it brief.

The first house was located about halfway between his office and his present apartment. A small brick Georgian, it was set on a tiny lot and smothered by overgrown boxwood hedges. The saleswoman, aptly named Julia Houser, was holding forth on the rate of appreciation. "So you see, it's a wonderful investment."

"I'm not particularly looking for an investment."

"There's a darling powder room tucked away under the stairs."

Jax, holding the baby, dutifully followed Ms. Houser through the house, from basement to two-car garage. "Central vacuum system," the woman said. "Your wife will love that."

Jax nodded glumly. Hetty said nothing. Her arms were crossed over her breasts.

"Why don't we look at the other place," he said, which was a little more polite than, "No thanks, no way, not interested."

The second house was located off Bell's Mill Road, which ran parallel to the Intracoastal Waterway. Most of the original homes had been built for weekenders. Summer homes. The one being shown was one of the oldest, which had been added on to with no particular thought as to design.

He liked it. There was nothing neat or orderly about it, yet something about the place appealed to him.

Hetty wandered around to the backyard, where at

one time someone had attempted to start a garden. Or had started one and then neglected it.

There were plenty of flaws, and to her credit, the saleswoman pointed them out. A section of rotting banister beside the back steps. A few porch boards that would need replacing.

"All the windows need reputtying, or you could replace them with double-paned windows."

"Hmm," was Jax's comment.

"It's only about thirty minutes from downtown Norfolk. Bell's Mill to Cedar to Dominion will take you right to the center of town. Actually, it's the best of both worlds, if you like a quiet neighborhood."

He liked a quiet neighborhood. Funny thing—he'd never realized before how bored he'd been with the Ghent area where he currently lived. Populated largely by professionals, it was considered highly fashionable, yet he'd never felt the least attachment to either the place or the people.

While he wasn't a hermit, he was not particularly social. Now and then he went out with a woman, but seldom more than once a week, and never over an extended period of time. The larger social gatherings he avoided altogether whenever possible.

"Shall we go inside? I think you'll like the kitchen, it's been modernized. The walls throughout the house are wood, but they can be painted."

Hetty fell in love with the house, but sensibly kept her opinion to herself. It was Jax's decision. By the time he moved in—*if* he moved in—she'd be back in Oklahoma, working out some arrangement to get back in the good graces of her family without totally losing her independence. There would have to be trade-offs, and Hetty told herself she was looking forward to getting started.

Funny thing, though, she had to remind herself over and over again of what it was she was going back for.

The real estate saleswoman was clearly puzzled by Hetty's role in all this. After the first few remarks directed her way, which Hetty referred to Jax, the woman ignored her.

They discussed schools. They discussed shopping areas. Sunny was growing restless, and Hetty took her outside and sat on the back porch in the late-afternoon sunshine. It was cold, but not unpleasant. In fact, it was entirely too pleasant. Too easy to dream.

You've had your dream, Henrietta. Now, go dig out this baby's bottle and do what you're being paid to do.

When Jax and Julia Houser came outside again, Sunny was almost asleep. Being around people stimulated her. Being outside where it was cool and quiet had the opposite effect.

"It's been a busy day, hasn't it, sugar-britches," Hetty murmured. "I have an idea you'll be spending a lot more time out here."

Screened in, it would make an ideal place for Sunny's playpen in a few months. Jax could work on his papers in that big room with all the windows. On weekends, he could work on his boat, while Rosie or someone like her brought Sunny out here on the back porch or maybe even down to the waterfront to watch the boats go by.

"Wake up, time to go."

"I wasn't asleep," Hetty mumbled drowsily. She had wedged herself in a corner with both knees propped up so that Sunny, asleep on her lap, couldn't take a tumble.

And besides, she really hadn't been asleep, she'd only been dreaming....

At first glance the boat was ugly. Hetty tried and failed to come up with an appropriate comment that wouldn't hurt Jax's feelings, because she knew how much he loved the old tub.

Her friend Billy's bass boat was purple with flecks of glitter embedded in the paint. The outboard was almost as big as the boat.

The *Lizzie-Linda* was propped up on a platform of criss-crossed timbers, her naked underside exposed for all the world to see. If there was a lick of paint on her anywhere, it didn't show.

"It's...interesting," was the best she could come up with.

"It's not an it, it's a she. Check out those lines. They don't build 'em like that anymore. Once I finish with the hull repairs, she'll be sound as a dollar. Wait'll you see her all painted up, with a new set of sails."

"Mercy, I can't imagine." She couldn't, not really, but she didn't have to imagine the excitement she saw in Jax's lean face. His eyes, usually guarded, fairly glowed with excitement.

She thought about something she'd heard once, about boys and their toys. This was no toy for Jax. It was a link to his roots, to his seagoing great-great-grandfather, whether or not he wanted to admit it.

They had dinner on the way home. The place wasn't fashionable, but Hetty felt comfortable, as it was one of those places where you knew just from looking at the outside that country-fried steak would be somewhere on the menu.

Jax ordered crab cakes. Hetty ordered the country-fried steak with green beans and sweet potatoes, dug out a teething biscuit for Sunny and fed her bits of the mashed vegetables.

They talked about the house. Jax wanted her opinion, and she gave it freely. The good and the bad.

"It's a wonderful old house. Lots of storage room, and believe me, you can never have enough of that. The yard has all kinds of possibilities. There's no way of knowing about the insulation, and with that high ceiling, heating it might be a problem. As for the roof, at least on the south side, it's going to need replacing pretty soon, judging from the way the shingles are curled. The basement smells like mildew, which means it probably floods when it rains hard."

Jax stared at her. "I thought you said you were no expert."

"I'm not. I've only lived in two houses in my entire life, but they were both old and ailing, and in both houses I was responsible for any maintenance that got done. I learned to recognize what could wait and what couldn't be put off another year. Basements can wait if they have to. Roofs can't. You'll end up with rotting eaves and falling ceilings.''

He smiled distractedly at the waitress when she topped off his coffee. Looking thoughtful, he stirred in twice the usual dose of sugar, leaving Hetty to wonder what he was thinking. The furrows between his eyebrows deepened. She hoped she hadn't added to his problems with her remarks about the house.

Still wondering, she let her gaze stray to his hair. It was growing shaggy, yet oddly enough it suited him. She thought about a biography she'd once read in the long, lonely years when reading had been her only form of recreation. George Patton, a famous general in World War II, had been a fascinating mixture of poet, philosopher and soldier.

She was beginning to think Jax was all of those and more.

It was after nine when they got back to the apartment. Sunny had fussed for a while and then fallen asleep. Hetty whispered, ''It's been a lovely day, Jax. I'd better get her ready for bed and warm up a bottle of water in case she needs a little encouragement to go back to sleep.'' She'd meant for him to leave.

Instead, he came inside and insisted on helping her. ''You go get her ready while I warm up the bottle. Then we'll talk.''

''Jax, I'm really tired.''

"I won't stay long, but I'd like your opinion on a few more things. Schools, day care—that sort of thing."

She thought those could probably wait a few years, but didn't say so. If the truth were known, there was nothing she would like better than to settle the baby, then curl up on that lumpy old sofa bed and talk about anything and everything...or nothing at all.

Jax recognized the signals she was sending out. He was good at reading body language, picking up hidden clues. He knew when an opponent was weakening, when to push, when to let nature take its course.

He made coffee while the bottle was warming, then tested the temperature on his wrist the way he'd seen Hetty do. If it had been up to him, he'd probably have run warm water out of the tap, but Hetty bought gallon jugs of the stuff and warmed it in a kettle. He trusted her judgment.

She tiptoed back into the kitchen. "I doubt if she'll need it, she settled right down after I changed her. Is that coffee I smell? Oh, good."

He smiled, trying not to gloat over the easy victory. He was determined to stay, possibly even all night. Turning away, he took out a carton of half-and-half and a wedge of cheese, which was about all there was in the tiny refrigerator. His momentary sense of triumph gave way to concern. "Look, we're going to have to do better than this. If you insist on cooking, you're going to need a real kitchen."

"Jax—"

"You can't even keep enough milk on hand in this thing."

"I don't drink it, and Sunny's formula comes in cans."

"You know what I mean. This place is—"

"Temporary," she said, and there was a familiar, implacable note in her voice. He'd heard it before, when she'd refused to come with him to Virginia.

He'd heard it again when she refused to accept a salary.

"Hetty, listen to me."

"No, you listen to me, Jax. I sat in on your interviews, and I'm satisfied with at least one of the candidates. Which means you won't need me much longer. I went with you to look at houses, and if you want my advice, you'll buy the one nearest your boat. It's not perfect, but you obviously love it. It suits you." He tried to interrupt, but she lifted her hand, palm out. "No, let me finish."

Crossing his arms over his chest, he leaned back against the cluttered, three-foot section of counter. "I'm listening."

It threw her off for a few seconds. Gamely, she picked up and went on to tell him that first of all, she had family depending on her. Secondly, she needed to find a job before all the Help Wanted signs disappeared.

"Because it's cyclical, you know. I read this book by a famous economist, and he said—"

"Hetty."

"He said that no matter who tried to take credit for

the economy, there were only a few things that could actually influ—''

''Hetty.''

''What?'' she wailed. ''I'm trying to explain why we both need to get on with our futures and stop wasting time with these...these stopgap measures.''

''You read too much. You also talk too much when you're trying to hide something.''

Her jaw fell, revealing the tiny chip in one of her incisors where she claimed to have tripped playing hopscotch. The second time she'd mentioned it she'd claimed to have had a bicycle accident.

He wondered how it had really happened....

Ten

Jax chose his words carefully. "Your priorities are family and a job. That's understandable."

"Of course it is, that's why—"

Ignoring her interruption, he baited his hook. "My priority is Sunny. She needs continuity. A real mother, not just a series of baby-sitters. So far, there's been damned little stability in her life. This book I've been reading, about raising kids, says stability in the early years is important."

This time she didn't interrupt. Her expression grew guarded, her body language clearly defensive, but he could tell she was curious, interested in the bait he was dangling.

He jiggled the line. "Can we agree on that much?"

"Yes—well, of course. Being uprooted at such an

early age can't be good for any child, but according to her résumé, Mrs. Clark stayed on at her last position for fourteen years, remember? She didn't leave until the youngest child went off to boarding school, which means she's steady and reliable.''

''It also means she's set in her ways. A baby needs someone who's flexible.''

''I thought you said a baby needed stability.''

''There's such a thing as flexible stability.'' At the mocking lift of her brows, he said, ''What, you don't agree?''

''I suppose…well, all right, then what about Rosie? She's not set in her ways, and she's certainly young enough to—''

''To find herself a man and get married.''

Hetty planted her fists on her hips. ''You're determined to make this as difficult as possible, aren't you? You asked for my opinion? I'll give it to you. Not one darned thing in this life is guaranteed. You just have to do the best you can and hope it all works out in the end. There's your flexible stability!''

''See? I knew you'd understand.''

If he'd wanted to get under her skin—and he had—that did the trick. Silver-gray eyes flashed fire. Spots of color burned high on her cheeks. ''Listen to me, Jackson Powers, if you're going to be any sort of a father at all to that poor child in there, you're the one who's going to have to learn to be more flexible!''

''So teach me.''

''So *what?*''

''Teach me to be flexible. Women are famous for being flexible, aren't they?''

Still militantly defensive, she allowed that some were, some weren't. Then, as if she'd suddenly grown too tired to stand guard any longer, she said, "Look, I know you have cause to be insecure, but—"

It was his turn to be indignant. "Insecure! What the devil gives you the idea I'm insecure?"

"Don't shout, you'll wake the baby. There, you see what I mean? Men always react that way when a woman gets too close to the truth. They get mad and start yelling and throwing things, or they—" She broke off and bit her lower lip.

"I thought your sainted husband was a paragon of all virtues." Cheap shot. It was a good thing he wasn't likely to face her in a lawsuit, because the woman could rock his boat quicker than anyone he'd ever known.

"He was," she said quietly. "My father wasn't. My stepson-in-law isn't."

Jax did a quick burn, thinking of how she must have gotten that chipped tooth, and God knows what else. If it was the stepson-in-law, he'd bury the jerk before he'd allow her anywhere near him again. "Hetty, your father's dead. Any man related by a string of modifiers can hardly be called family. Isn't it about time to cut your losses and start over? You might even try exercising some of that flexibility you accused me of lacking."

She took a deep, shaky breath, avoiding his eyes. Jax, a sense of triumph beginning to glow inside him like banked coals, cautioned himself against celebrating too soon. One lesson he'd learned early in life was that a man who played by the rules—a man who firmly believed in the rule of law—could be sucker-punched by someone who didn't know the first thing about how the game was played.

Come on, give in, sweetheart. You're teetering on the brink and you know it.

"I'm sorry about your family, Hetty. For what it's worth, mine didn't work out, either. We have that in common. It's not going to happen to Sunny, though, not as long as I have anything to say about it. My daughter's going to have it all."

"All right."

"A home, a dog, maybe even a cat. Santa Claus and the Easter Bunny—someone of her own to show up for parents' day at school. Someone to spoil her, to take care of her when she picks up a bug at school and comes home throwing up and feeling lousy. Someone to—"

"All right."

"Someone to—" He did a slow double take. "What?"

"I said, all right," Hetty repeated patiently. "I will. You've talked me into it."

"You *will?*"

"I just said so, didn't I?"

He barely refrained from grabbing her, whirling her around and shouting *whoopee,* or something equally applicable.

Still guarded, she said, "Do you want it in writing? Lawyers are big on contracts, so write one up and I'll sign it. But not," she stressed, "until I've read all the fine print."

Jax felt the starch drain out of his backbone. Braced

for a flat-out refusal, he'd had his first defensive volley all ready to fire. "Well, hey—that's great," he said, trying to keep from grinning too broadly.

He held out his arms.

She took a step back.

"Doesn't it even rate a kiss?"

Warily, she shook her head. "We need to get the rules spelled out and agreed to on both sides. No kissing. This is going to be strictly a business arrangement. Whatever happened in the past is—well, it's not going to happen again."

He narrowed a suspicious look at her. "What do you mean, it's not going to happen again? Hetty, be reasonable. It's too late to change the rules now. As my wife, you're going to be sleeping in my bed for the rest of your—"

"As your *what?*"

"My wife. What the devil did you think I was talking about?"

"Well…your employee. Instead of Rosie or Mrs. Clark. For flexible security—you know. For Sunny?"

Closing his eyes, Jax prayed briefly and inexpertly for patience. He had an idea he was going to need all he could lay his hands on for the next few decades. "Honey, I just asked you to marry me. You agreed. And let me remind you that a verbal contract can be as binding as a written one under the right circumstances."

Her jaw fell. He stared at the chipped tooth, clenched his fists and swore a silent oath that nothing would ever hurt her again, as long as it was within his power to prevent it.

Hetty felt behind her for a chair. Slowly she sat, her gaze never leaving his. "You did? I mean, it is?"

"I did, you did, and it is." This time there was no concealing his feelings. Triumph, tenderness, a welling of optimism he couldn't remember ever feeling before, at least not in a personal context.

"For Sunny's sake?"

"For Sunny's sake," he told her, knowing that wasn't the whole reason. He suspected it was no longer even a major part of it, but explanations could wait. "Look, it's a natural." He counted off the reasons on his fingers. "We get along well, we both care about Sunny's welfare, you don't have any real obligations, and Sunny and I have a definite need."

She thought about it. He watched the process, seeing the doubts arise, seeing her deal with them in order. If it was within his power, he would have slain all her dragons for her, but that was going to take time.

"It's going to work, you'll see," was the best he could do for the moment. She had a past to come to terms with, just as he did. Strange thing, though. His own no longer seemed relevant. Maybe he'd outgrown it.

Or maybe his future had finally overtaken the past.

The sofa bed creaked. It was lumpy, its coarse plaid upholstery ugly as homemade sin, but neither of them noticed. It could've been eiderdown covered in silk brocade for all the difference it made. Once Hetty had accepted the idea that no matter how convenient it happened to be, theirs was definitely *not* going to be the proverbial marriage of convenience, she'd laid down her arms without further protest.

What followed had been inevitable, considering the overwhelming attraction that had been growing between them ever since he'd first turned to meet a pair of guileless silver-gray eyes.

"We've got to get you out of this place," Jax muttered, having bumped his head twice on the arms of the too-short sofa.

"Call Mrs. Houser and ask her how soon you can close on the house."

"You want that one? The Bell's Mill Road place?"

"Don't you?" Momentarily sated from having made love, Hetty toyed with the tuft of hair surrounding his nipple. The small brown bud tightened, and she smiled with a growing sense of power. He might not love her, but he wasn't as unaffected as he wanted her to believe.

"It's probably the most practical choice," he conceded.

"Sunny needs a yard to play in."

"And you need a garden to dig in. I saw you eyeing that overgrown weed patch in the back."

"You need to be closer to your boat."

"Our boat," he corrected, covering her hand with his and moving it lower on his body. "In case you don't realize it, you're dealing with high explosives, woman."

"Is that a warning?"

"Call it a promise."

"I'll hold you to it," she purred, rejoicing in the sexual banter that was so new to her. There was no longer any doubt in her mind that she loved him. Hadn't been in a long time. If he couldn't love her in return, then she would settle for his trust, his respect and his affection. In time it might even suffice.

He nuzzled her throat. "Mmm, you smell good," he growled.

"Soap and shampoo."

"And warm, sexy woman."

It was all the aphrodisiac they needed. Jax said, "We might as well take advantage of the opportunity while Sunny's asleep."

So they did.

And as Sunny slept through the night, there was ample opportunity to explore what for Hetty was a brand-new world. A world of sweet, mindless passion.

To his amazement, it was the same for Jax. He even said as much. "Honey, you know—well, you've probably guessed that you're not the, uh, the first woman in my life."

Gravely she said, "I'd suspected there might have been a few. The fact that you have a daughter is a dead giveaway."

"Yeah, well, I just wanted you to know that it's never—oh, hell, this sounds like one of those Valentine clichés. It's never been like this for me before." The words came out all in a rush. "What I mean is…"

Taking pity on him, she covered his lips with her fingers. "I know what you mean. It is sort of—well, overwhelming, isn't it? All I have to do is look at you and—"

"I know what you mean. Me, too."

He looked at her, and she looked right back, and then they laughed and fell into each other's arms. Again.

The phone call came just as the sky was beginning to turn a pinkish-gray in the east. Hetty, used to sleeping with one ear open for a baby, rolled off the sofa, reached for the phone and mumbled into the receiver.

"Is that you? Hetty, you sound weird."

"Jeannie, what's wrong?"

"Why do you automatically think something's wrong every time I decide to give you a call?"

"For one thing," Hetty replied dryly, rubbing her eyes with one fist, "you've never called before. For another, it's the middle of the night."

"Well, pardon me! I should've known you didn't really care about Robert. Sorry I bothered—"

"Jeannie! Don't hang up. Wait—just give me a minute to get my eyes open."

Jax flopped over onto his side. His arm fell across her lap. He mumbled something, and Hetty whispered for him to go back to sleep.

"Who're you talking to? Hetty, is someone there with you? Is it a man? Are you—God, I should've guessed when you didn't come back home!"

"Jeannie, what's wrong? You said something about Robert. Is he all right?"

"A lot you care!"

"Dammit, I do care! Stop playing games and just tell me what's wrong."

"Oooh, listen to who's cursing now. Saint Henrietta-who-can-do-no-wrong. Boy, was Nicky ever right about you. You sure didn't waste much time picking your next victim, did you?''

Hetty took a deep breath. She'd dealt with Jeannie's spite for years, telling herself it was only natural for a daughter to resent the woman who took her mother's place in her father's life.

By now Jax was fully awake. He eased out from behind her and padded, naked as the day he was born, to the bathroom. Hetty, listening to Jeannie go on and on about babies who never sleep and husbands who refuse to help with the housework and who go into debt to buy a brand-new pickup truck, admired his physique. If he'd been short, balding and pudgy, she probably would have admired him almost as much. It was the sum total of who he was she'd fallen in love with, not the sum total of what he looked like.

Although the looks didn't hurt at all, she had to admit.

"Rub his gums," she said into the phone. "If you dip your finger in ice cream and rub his gums, he'll stop crying. It's the crying that makes him swallow air, and that hurts his little tummy. Oh, and if you drag that old porch rocker into the bedroom and rock him while you're rubbing his gums, he'll fall asleep and then you can go back to bed.''

She listened to more complaints. Jax reappeared, stepped into the kitchen, and she heard the sound of the microwave. "Look, I can't help you with Nicky— Jeannie, be fair. You know I can't just—''

She accepted a cup of reheated coffee, well diluted with cream. Jax touched her head, smoothing her hair, and then began collecting his clothes. He had yet to put on a stitch. It was hard to concentrate on Jeannie's laundry list of complaints with all that glorious masculinity parading back and forth in front of her. She suspected he was doing it deliberately. As if she might need reminding of her promise to marry him.

"Because I can't, that's all. Jeannie, do you have any idea how much it costs to fly from here to Oklahoma?"

She nodded her thanks when Jax spread his shirt over her naked shoulders, realizing for the first time that his wasn't the only bare body in the room.

Mercy. If the sight of hers affected him the way the sight of his affected her, they were both in trouble.

"No, I can't send you any money. Jeannie, be reasonable. Nicky is going to have to stick with a job longer than three days, and you're both going to have to grow up. You have a son to think about now. Remember what your grandmother used to say about making your bed and sleeping in it?"

She held the phone away from her ear. The sound of an outraged voice came through clearly. After a while she broke in and said, "No, Jeannie, I'm not lecturing you, I'm just trying to help you understand—"

Before she realized what he was up to, Jax removed the phone from her hand. "Jeannie? Jackson Powers here. I'm Hetty's fiancé—yes, that's right. Hey, don't feel sorry for me, I've had a rough time trying to talk her into marrying me, but—yes, I know she's bossy. I can handle it."

There was a long pause, during which Hetty started

in awe at the man she had just agreed to marry—
although he'd never actually got around to asking her.
She listened while he talked about Sunny, and about
swapping baby pictures. He talked about the value of
continuing education, which for Jeannie would mean
getting her GED first.

And then he said, "If you'll promise to do it and
make the arrangements, I'll pay for it. But I have to
have some assurance you'll go through with it. It
takes patience and a certain degree of maturity, but
Hetty assures me you've got what it takes."

Hetty rolled her eyes. A few moments later Jax
hung up the phone, and she lit into him. "Would you
mind telling me what that was all about?"

"Mostly about fence mending. About your peace
of mind. If I'm going to have to live with you, I
deserve—"

"You're not going to have to do anything, as far
as I'm concerned. We can just unsign this so-called
verbal contract right now, if—"

He laid a finger over her lips. "Shh, don't get your
bloomers in a wad."

She removed his finger, glaring up at him. "That's
a disgusting expression!"

"I thought you might like it, you being a country
girl and all." The corners of her mouth quivered before she could clamp her lips together. Dead giveaway. He was on to her now. "May I remind you that
once a verbal contract is signed—"

"You can't sign a verbal contract, and even if you
could, I haven't signed anything yet, remember?"

"Sure you have. You gave me your word, remember?"

"Yes, but that doesn't mean you have to take on my whole family."

"No? Isn't that just what you did when you married Gus?"

"Well, yes, but that was different."

"You fell head over heels for the guy, is that it?"

She pulled his shirt more closely around her throat, wishing she weren't exposed from the hips down. Dignity was hard to achieve when a woman was half-naked, still rumpled from having made mad, passionate love. "I...I learned to love him, yes."

"You're taking on my whole family. Do you think you might learn to love me? In time, I mean. I wouldn't expect it right away."

That was when the whole game fell apart. She lifted her eyes to meet his, and no power on earth could keep her feelings from shining out like a beacon in the night.

Jax whispered her name on a sigh and sank down beside her. Given the deplorable condition of the springs, she was toppled against him. He took full advantage. "You do love me, don't you? No, don't even try to deny it. I might be lousy at a lot of things, but when it comes to reading people, I'm an expert."

"If you're such an expert, how come you're just now figuring that out?" she grumbled, hiding a smile.

It wasn't until much later that she got her answer. "I was afraid to hope. Afraid to trust. I guess when it comes to love, I'm still a rank beginner."

"I have a feeling you'll be a fast learner, though."

"With the right teacher, there's no telling what I can do," he vowed, his voice earnest, his eyes alight with all the things she'd never dared hope to find there.

"Want to know why I fell in love with you?" she whispered.

"Does telling break the spell?"

"No, that's wishing on a star."

"No stars, but just to be on the safe side, don't look out the window."

If a heart could burst with love, hers came close. "Almost from the first I began to notice things about you I've never seen in another man. The way you looked so stiff and arrogant even though you were obviously out of your element."

"That's it? You love me because I'm stiff and arrogant?"

"Well, I noticed you first because your baby needed changing, but pretty soon I got interested in more than Sunny. Once I discovered that inside you're soft as a marshmallow, it was all over for me."

Flopping over onto his back, Jax covered his eyes with an arm. "Don't even think such a thing. If word leaks out, I'll never win another case."

"That's another thing. You have a sense of humor. Gus was the dearest man in the world, but he never laughed. I need to laugh, Jax. I want to be able to laugh and cry and not have to hold it all in."

His arms came around her, and she hurried to finish what she had to say before she lost her train of thought. "I tried not to at first. Love you, that is.

Because I kept telling myself I had a life back in Oklahoma—a family who needed me.''

"You can go back anytime you want to, sweetheart, only not without me. Sooner or later the kids need to get to know each other. They're sort of cousins or something, aren't they?''

"That might be stretching it, but…why not?''

"Yeah, why not? Hell, I'll even take on Jeannie and that jerk she's married to, if it'll make you happy.''

Eyes glowing, Hetty rolled over to lie on top of him "*You* make me happy. *Sunny* makes me happy. Everything else is gravy.''

* * * * *

*Be sure to look for Jackson's
great-great-grandfather's story*

THE PAPER MARRIAGE

*by Bronwyn Williams,
the pseudonym for Dixie Browning
and her sister Mary Williams.*

*Available in August 2000 from
Harlequin Historicals.*

If you enjoyed what you just read,
then we've got an offer you can't resist!

Take 2 bestselling love stories FREE!

Plus get a FREE surprise gift!

Clip this page and mail it to Silhouette Reader Service™

IN U.S.A.	IN CANADA
3010 Walden Ave.	P.O. Box 609
P.O. Box 1867	Fort Erie, Ontario
Buffalo, N.Y. 14240-1867	L2A 5X3

YES! Please send me 2 free Silhouette Desire® novels and my free surprise gift. Then send me 6 brand-new novels every month, which I will receive months before they're available in stores. In the U.S.A., bill me at the bargain price of $3.12 plus 25¢ delivery per book and applicable sales tax, if any*. In Canada, bill me at the bargain price of $3.49 plus 25¢ delivery per book and applicable taxes**. That's the complete price and a savings of over 10% off the cover prices—what a great deal! I understand that accepting the 2 free books and gift places me under no obligation ever to buy any books. I can always return a shipment and cancel at any time. Even if I never buy another book from Silhouette, the 2 free books and gift are mine to keep forever. So why not take us up on our invitation. You'll be glad you did!

225 SEN CNFA
326 SEN CNFC

Name	(PLEASE PRINT)	
Address	Apt.#	
City	State/Prov.	Zip/Postal Code

* Terms and prices subject to change without notice. Sales tax applicable in N.Y.
** Canadian residents will be charged applicable provincial taxes and GST.
   All orders subject to approval. Offer limited to one per household.
   ® are registered trademarks of Harlequin Enterprises Limited.

DES99   ©1998 Harlequin Enterprises Limited

January 2000
HER FOREVER MAN
#1267 by Leanne Banks
Lone Star Families: The Logans

February 2000
A BRIDE FOR JACKSON POWERS
#1273 by Dixie Browning
The Passionate Powers

March 2000
A COWBOY'S SECRET
#1279 by Anne McAllister
Code of the West

April 2000
LAST DANCE
#1285 by Cait London
Freedom Valley

May 2000
DR. IRRESISTIBLE
#1291 by Elizabeth Bevarly
From Here to Maternity

June 2000
TOUGH TO TAME
#1297 by Jackie Merritt

MAN OF THE MONTH

For twenty years Silhouette has been giving you
the ultimate in romantic reads. Come join the
celebration as some of your favorite authors
help celebrate our anniversary with the most
sensual, emotional love stories ever!

Available at your favorite retail outlet.

Silhouette®
Where love comes alive™

Visit us at www.romance.net

SDMOM00

SILHOUETTE'S 20TH ANNIVERSARY CONTEST
OFFICIAL RULES
NO PURCHASE NECESSARY TO ENTER

1. To enter, follow directions published in the offer to which you are responding. Contest begins 1/1/00 and ends on 8/24/00 (the "Promotion Period"). Method of entry may vary. Mailed entries must be postmarked by 8/24/00, and received by 8/31/00.

2. During the Promotion Period, the Contest may be presented via the Internet. Entry via the Internet may be restricted to residents of certain geographic areas that are disclosed on the Web site. To enter via the Internet, if you are a resident of a geographic area in which Internet entry is permissible, follow the directions displayed on-line, including typing your essay of 100 words or fewer telling us "Where In The World Your Love Will Come Alive." On-line entries must be received by 11:59 p.m. Eastern Standard time on 8/24/00. Limit one e-mail entry per person, household and e-mail address per day, per presentation. If you are a resident of a geographic area in which entry via the Internet is permissible, you may, in lieu of submitting an entry on-line, enter by mail, by hand-printing your name, address, telephone number and contest number/name on an 8"x 11" plain piece of paper and telling us in 100 words or fewer "Where In The World Your Love Will Come Alive," and mailing via first-class mail to: Silhouette 20th Anniversary Contest, (in the U.S.) P.O. Box 9069, Buffalo, NY 14269-9069; (In Canada) P.O. Box 637, Fort Erie, Ontario, Canada L2A 5X3. Limit one 8"x 11" mailed entry per person, household and e-mail address per day. On-line and/or 8"x 11" mailed entries received from persons residing in geographic areas in which Internet entry is not permissible will be disqualified. No liability is assumed for lost, late, incomplete, inaccurate, nondelivered or misdirected mail, or misdirected e-mail, for technical, hardware or software failures of any kind, lost or unavailable network connection, or failed, incomplete, garbled or delayed computer transmission or any human error which may occur in the receipt or processing of the entries in the contest.

3. Essays will be judged by a panel of members of the Silhouette editorial and marketing staff based on the following criteria:

   Sincerity (believability, credibility)—50%

   Originality (freshness, creativity)—30%

   Aptness (appropriateness to contest ideas)—20%

   Purchase or acceptance of a product offer does not improve your chances of winning. In the event of a tie, duplicate prizes will be awarded.

4. All entries become the property of Harlequin Enterprises Ltd., and will not be returned. Winner will be determined no later than 10/31/00 and will be notified by mail. Grand Prize winner will be required to sign and return Affidavit of Eligibility within 15 days of receipt of notification. Noncompliance within the time period may result in disqualification and an alternative winner may be selected. All municipal, provincial, federal, state and local laws and regulations apply. Contest open only to residents of the U.S. and Canada who are 18 years of age or older, and is void wherever prohibited by law. Internet entry is restricted solely to residents of those geographical areas in which Internet entry is permissible. Employees of Torstar Corp., their affiliates, agents and members of their immediate families are not eligible. Taxes on the prizes are the sole responsibility of winners. Entry and acceptance of any prize offered constitutes permission to use winner's name, photograph or other likeness for the purposes of advertising, trade and promotion on behalf of Torstar Corp. without further compensation to the winner, unless prohibited by law. Torstar Corp and D.L. Blair, Inc., their parents, affiliates and subsidiaries, are not responsible for errors in printing or electronic presentation of contest or entries. In the event of printing or other errors which may result in unintended prize values or duplication of prizes, all affected contest materials or entries shall be null and void. If for any reason the Internet portion of the contest is not capable of running as planned, including infection by computer virus, bugs, tampering, unauthorized intervention, fraud, technical failures, or any other causes beyond the control of Torstar Corp. which corrupt or affect the administration, secrecy, fairness, integrity or proper conduct of the contest, Torstar Corp. reserves the right, at its sole discretion, to disqualify any individual who tampers with the entry process and to cancel, terminate, modify or suspend the contest or the Internet portion thereof. In the event of a dispute regarding an on-line entry, the entry will be deemed submitted by the authorized holder of the e-mail account submitted at the time of entry. Authorized account holder is defined as the natural person who is assigned to an e-mail address by an Internet access provider, on-line service provider or other organization that is responsible for arranging e-mail address for the domain associated with the submitted e-mail address.

5. Prizes: Grand Prize—a $10,000 vacation to anywhere in the world. Travelers (at least one must be 18 years of age or older) or parent or guardian if one traveler is a minor, must sign and return a Release of Liability prior to departure. Travel must be completed by December 31, 2001, and is subject to space and accommodations availability. Two hundred (200) Second Prizes—a two-book limited edition autographed collector set from one of the Silhouette Anniversary authors: Nora Roberts, Diana Palmer, Linda Howard or Annette Broadrick (value $10.00 each set). All prizes are valued in U.S. dollars.

6. For a list of winners (available after 10/31/00), send a self-addressed, stamped envelope to: Harlequin Silhouette 20th Anniversary Winners, P.O. Box 4200, Blair, NE 68009-4200.

Contest sponsored by Torstar Corp., P.O. Box 9042, Buffalo, NY 14269-9042.

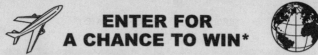

ENTER FOR
A CHANCE TO WIN*

Silhouette's 20th Anniversary Contest

Tell Us Where in the World
You Would Like *Your* Love To Come Alive...
And We'll Send the Lucky Winner There!

Silhouette wants to take you wherever
your happy ending can come true.

Here's how to enter: Tell us, in 100 words or less,
where you want to go to make your love come alive!

In addition to the grand prize, there will be 200
runner-up prizes, collector's-edition book sets
autographed by one of the Silhouette anniversary
authors: **Nora Roberts, Diana Palmer,
Linda Howard** or **Annette Broadrick**.

DON'T MISS YOUR CHANCE TO WIN!
ENTER NOW! No Purchase Necessary

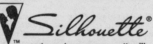

Silhouette®
Where love comes alive™

Name:

Address:

City: State/Province:

Zip/Postal Code:

Mail to Harlequin Books: **In the U.S.**: P.O. Box 9069, Buffalo, NY
14269-9069; **In Canada**: P.O. Box 637, Fort Erie, Ontario, L4A 5X3